"SOMEDAY YOU'LL REALIZE THAT NOT EVERY RELATIONSHIP IS A JAIL CELL."

"No one was meant to live alone," Jason said. "And, I might add, for a lady who wants nothing to do with men, you wear rather sexy underwear. It made me think I wasn't the only one who had hopes for this evening. But there won't be any more evenings like this. I'm too old to tolerate being thwarted very often, and too young to resign myself to your celibate wishes."

Lorna thought they might still have one or two evenings together. She tried to breathe slowly, amazed at the depth of her hurt. They'd been so close, it was difficult to believe he could say goodbye this easily.

She forced herself to speak levelly. "I'm sorry," she said, wondering at the same time what she was apologizing for.

"Apologies," he said, "are not what I want."

CANDLELIGHT ECSTASY ROMANCES®

LOVE'S SECRET GARDEN

Nona Gamel

A CANDLELIGHT ECSTASY ROMANCE®

Published by
Dell Publishing Co., Inc.
1 Dag Hammarskjold Plaza
New York, New York 10017

Dell® TM 681510, Dell Publishing Co., Inc.
Candlelight Ecstasy Romance®, 1,203,540, is a registered
trademark of Dell Publishing Co., Inc., New York, New York.

ISBN: 0-440-15021-3

Printed in the United States of America
First printing—August 1984

To Our Readers:

We have been delighted with your enthusiastic response to Candlelight Ecstasy Romances®, and we thank you for the interest you have shown in this exciting series.

In the upcoming months we will continue to present the distinctive, sensuous love stories you have come to expect only from Ecstasy. We look forward to bringing you many more books from your favorite authors and also the very finest work from new authors of contemporary romantic fiction.

As always, we are striving to present the unique, absorbing love stories that you enjoy most—books that are more than ordinary romance. Your suggestions and comments are always welcome. Please write to us at the address below.

Sincerely,

The Editors
Candlelight Romances
1 Dag Hammarskjold Plaza
New York, New York 10017

CHAPTER ONE

Lorna hissed in frustration as she slammed down the telephone receiver and swung her desk chair around to face the window. At nine in the morning the campus of Crowley College was still peaceful, and her view of the marble courtyard around the bronze fountain was unobstructed by the crowds of students that would appear there later in the day. Today, even the blue skies overhead, the low clouds on the horizon, and the faint sound of falling water that reached her office were insufficient to soothe her. Why, oh, why, had the sophomore class chosen the Woebegone Werewolves for their outdoor summer concert? Surely there were other groups equally raucous and somewhat more approachable.

When letters and telephone calls to the man reputed to be their manager had gone unanswered, Lorna had resorted to a direct assault. A series of alternately pleading and demanding calls to their recording company had finally produced the home telephone number of the group's leader, Beo, but Lorna's sense of triumph was short-lived. Beo had apparently been deafened by his own music, and Lorna suspected his brains had been scrambled as well. After her fifth shriek of "I'm calling from Crowley College. We want to book you for a June concert," Lorna had rather meanly suggested, still at her most ear-piercing volume, that Beo turn off his stereo. Instead, he had turned the phone over to someone else with a muttered, "Find out what she wants."

His unnamed substitute, after contributing several "huh's" had held the phone away from his mouth to announce quite audibly, "Some chick wants to put you in her book," and at that point she had summarily terminated the conversation.

"Lorna Phillips never gives up," she reminded herself aloud, mentally reviewing her most prized victories. There was the Brazilian novelist whom she had snared while he was negotiating film rights in Hollywood, the reclusive violinist she had tracked down at his health club, and the "retired" folk singer she had lured to Crowley by describing the dean of women's rather extensive collection of antique dulcimers. Could she do less for the sophomore class? After all, she didn't have to enjoy the concert, just arrange it.

Fortunately, they were not a local group, or her pride would have forced her to make a trip to at least one of their homes. She gnawed thoughtfully on a pencil eraser, her gray eyes fixed unseeing on the paneled wall of her office. As always before trying to arrange an appearance on campus, she had researched the Woebegone Werewolves as best she could. As inspiration struck she rifled through the manila folder of clippings and articles. There it was! Beo actually had a mother, poor thing, who lived in Nevada. Lorna reread the interview quickly, conferred with the information operator, and within minutes was explaining her problem to a surprisingly soft-spoken woman. Armed with the telephone number of the group's new manager, she was finally able to complete arrangements. "I just hope those sophomores know what they're doing," she murmured as she noted the concert for the campus events calendar.

"Have you had a bad morning already?" Fran from the admissions office stuck her head in the door. "Your hair's all poking out in tufts."

Lorna obediently smoothed down her short, honey-blond hair. Her current hair style—straight hair that curved in just below her rather square chin—was supposed to be trouble-free, but somehow the sleek look she had desired eluded her.

"Never mind." Fran shrugged, her coffee tilting precariously in the flowered mug. "I'm just jealous. Messy hair makes you look even sexier, but it makes me look like I've narrowly escaped electrocution."

"And to think I always wanted curly hair like yours." Lorna laughed. "Bring your coffee in and sit down for a minute. I deserve a break."

"Where's Susan? Has she had the baby?" Lorna's glamorous secretary, now eight months pregnant, had always been the object of much interest in the administration building, but the development of an office pool for her baby's arrival had considerably increased the attention given her.

"No, she's picking up Jason Coulter at the airport."

"Not *the* Jason Coulter! I guess I'm out of touch. How did you ever get him here? Not that Crowley College isn't Mecca," Fran added hastily.

"With no trouble," Lorna said smugly. Jason Coulter's reading had been so easy to arrange that she had given him very little thought since then. "It seems he's an old friend of President Arnold's, and he has other friends in the area too. I guess he was glad to have an excuse to come out here. Even in May, I doubt that Vermont can compete with California. I just had to promise we'd keep it low key. No publicity off campus."

11

"I would have offered to pick him up at the airport if I'd known," Fran said wistfully.

Lorna laughed. "Not a chance. Susan had her car specially washed and waxed for the occasion. She assured me nothing would stop her from meeting his plane."

"Another fan, huh? I'm not a poetry reader like you, but I've read a little of his work and I think I could become addicted." The ringing of a distant telephone interrupted her. "That may be mine. See you."

Reminded of the upcoming reading, Lorna set aside the Werewolves' folder with a sigh of relief and pulled out the file labeled Coulter. A call to Maintenance to ensure that the lectern and microphone were set up would probably be a good idea, she decided. If she knew how tall he was, it would save time later.

She browsed through the newspaper clippings in the folder, many of which had been supplied by the students who had requested him as the May guest lecturer. Married at eighteen, divorced at nineteen, never remarried. A man after her own heart. Gave up corporation law at the height of his career, apparently suffering from some sort of mid-life crisis, and two years later he had published his first volume of poetry, *A Dandelion for the Princess*. Compared to the work of Dylan Thomas, his poetry was said to appeal to both young and old readers. His first book had sold out immediately and Lorna, usually diligent in becoming familiar with visitors' work, had given up after several attempts to find a copy.

One article in the folder was devoted entirely to the rural Vermont house Coulter had designed himself. Lorna repressed a sigh at a picture of the elegant cedar structure almost hidden by trees. The man knew how to use his money, which he probably had plenty of, she thought. Her own house was similar in design but of

12

course much smaller and somehow less cleanly conceived.

Nowhere in the file was there a photograph of the poet himself. By keeping his appearance something of a mystery, he was able to maintain his privacy. With a faint "Aha" she pounced on a personal interview which began, traditionally enough, with a description of the interviewee. About six feet tall, clad in neat gray slacks and a blue Norwegian sweater. Dark, deepset blue eyes with rather large pupils, dark hair with sunstreaks and traces of gray, a few lines at the corners of his eyes. Thick black eyebrows, aquiline nose, firm chin. "And so on," she murmured, jotting down "6 ft." on a slip of paper. Apparently the lack of photographs didn't indicate any physical flaw.

How would it feel to read someone else's view of your appearance? Idly, Lorna fantasized her own description. About five feet five inches, slender but full-breasted, wearing a sleeveless Liberty print dress and high-heeled sandals. Gray eyes and short, thick blond hair. Square chin, full lower lip. A typical Midwestern farm girl. She frowned. It would be fun to be dark and sultry instead of so Nordic and healthy-looking. With half her attention devoted to clearing her desk, she dialed Maintenance and completed the arrangements. The phone rang as she hung up and she picked it up reflexively, smiling as she heard her sister's voice.

"Lorna? It's Beth. Would you like to come over for dinner tonight?"

"Sorry, love, I've got the reading and dinner for Jason Coulter tonight."

"Tomorrow then?" Ever since Lorna's divorce a year ago, Beth had devoted herself to finding a suitable man for her sister, and she probably had invited someone eligible to dinner.

13

"I'm having dinner with Brian tomorrow."

"You know you aren't serious about him. When are you going to settle down with just one man?"

"Never, I hope," Lorna said with forced lightness. "I'm enjoying myself."

"Okay." Beth sighed heavily after a lengthy pause. "Call if you get lonely."

"Of course." The conversation ended with the noisy return of Beth's children from swimming lessons, and Lorna went back to her work with a feeling of relief. Beth wouldn't be satisfied until she had remarried, and a year after her divorce, Lorna was still no closer to settling down. Having been contentedly married herself for nearly twenty years, Beth had no idea of the exhilaration Lorna was experiencing now that the pain of losing Ward, her ex-husband, was gone. Her own person at last, no longer struggling to conform to the tastes of a man on whose approval she depended, Lorna felt she would be crazy to give up what she had won with such difficulty.

The phone rang again and she answered absently, "Lorna Phillips."

"This is Jason Coulter." The slightly rough baritone voice was intensely masculine and very commanding. She could imagine its tones resounding in a corporate boardroom. "I'm calling from Samaritan Hospital."

"Oh, my God! Was there an accident?" Lorna's stomach twisted unpleasantly.

"Don't worry. Your secretary is in the delivery room and doing fine."

As relief washed over her, Lorna felt a bubble of mirth rising in her throat.

"It appears she thought she might be going into labor last night, but she neglected to say anything to her husband. And I understand, the baby wasn't expected for another two weeks. Anyway, my plane was a little late

14

and what with one thing and another, she almost ran into a bus on the way out of the parking lot. So, discretion seeming the better part of valor, I insisted on driving her to the hospital, which I did while she breathed heavily on my neck from the backseat."

"Welcome to Crowley College." Lorna choked back her laughter.

"It's been an eventful morning," Jason Coulter said evenly. "I have directions to the campus, and I have Susan's car."

"She waxed it specially for you," Lorna informed him solemnly, struggling to control an attack of giggles.

"It looks very nice." The voice was dry. "I called because I thought you might want to notify her husband. Do you think I should bring her car to the campus?"

"That would be a big help, if you really don't mind. Just park it in front of the administration building and I'll get it back to her later. Then come on up to my office and I'll take you to your guest cottage." She was all business now, and a little embarrassed. "I'm sorry you've had such a disorganized arrival."

"On the contrary, if I'm correctly interpreting those muffled sounds you've been making, I can entertain my friends with this story very successfully. I wouldn't have missed it for the world."

"I don't know," Lorna said doubtfully. "What strikes me as funny is not always universally appreciated."

"A pity. I'll expect to see you soon then."

Lorna dispatched Susan's husband to the hospital with instructions to call with any news. A second call to Fran ensured that word of the impending birth would spread around the building. She realized suddenly that the secretary hired to fill in for Susan was not due for another two weeks. Since she herself typed with only two fingers, not having a secretary would really slow her down.

A quick trip down the carpeted stairs to the personnel office yielded her a promise that they would either have the new secretary start earlier or find someone else to fill in. Back in her office, Lorna made several phone calls, then settled back into her comfortable indigo desk chair. The sudden and rapidly shifting emotions she had experienced when talking to Jason Coulter had left her feeling slightly dizzy. With one toe anchored firmly in the pale blue carpet, she idly swung her chair back and forth, her head resting against the back. What a sexy voice the man had. She looked forward to attending his poetry reading. With her eyes closed, and drifting into fantasy, she imagined his voice murmuring an intimate poem of love.

"Busy day?"

The words were hardly the sweet endearments she had been imagining, but she recognized their source immediately. She swung her chair back to face the door and stood up, afraid the slim dark-haired man standing there might have read her thoughts. And he easily could have, she realized suddenly as their eyes met—her flushed cheeks, shining eyes, and faintly heaving breasts probably announced to any careful observer that she had been lost in an erotic daydream. There was some consolation in knowing that he couldn't possibly have guessed his role in the fantasy.

She extended her hand, admiring his beautifully tailored sport coat and subtle silk tie.

"I'm Lorna Phillips. I'm glad you're finally here after all your adventures, Mr. Coulter."

"Jason," he corrected her, grasping her hand firmly for a moment and then releasing it. The newspaper description had been reasonably accurate, but it hadn't really prepared her for the depth of his eyes, which were an unusual dark shade of blue. They regarded her closely as, at her gesture, he sat down in the chair across her desk.

16

"I'm somewhat relieved to be here myself, I must admit, although I do feel I acquitted myself rather well."

"It's the price of fame." Lorna smiled. "If Susan hadn't been one of your most ardent fans, it never would have happened."

"I wonder. Is there a coffee shop where I could get a doughnut? For some reason, I'm as hungry as a lumberjack."

"Stress," Lorna said wisely. "When you called I envisioned a horrible pileup on the freeway, and I've been starving ever since. I'll walk over to the coffee house with you. It will help you learn your way around a little. Then when we both have our strength back I'll take you to your cottage."

"Wonderful."

"Let me just duck down the hall to leave word where I'll be," she said, slipping out the door. What was the matter with her, anyway, fantasizing about a man because she liked his voice over the phone? Although in his case his appearance certainly fulfilled the promise of his baritone voice. After leaving her message with Fran, who rolled her eyes dramatically at the thought of coffee with Jason Coulter, Lorna walked quickly back to her office to find the poet in front of the window.

"I'm surprised you get any work done with a view like this. Up here I feel like a Spanish grandee looking haughtily out on my marble courtyard."

"How would one thousand students in sloganed T-shirts fit into your vision?"

He shrugged. "Peasants cheering my munificence under the balcony. Or off to a special mass in honor of my birthday."

"How about peasants in revolt, about to plunder your castle and burn your tapestries?"

17

"Not my style at all. Perhaps you're more blood-thirsty?"

"I guess I just don't believe in romantic visions."

He looked at her gravely. "We all need romantic visions."

Lorna shook her head. "There's always the danger of confusing fantasy and reality, or of wishing the two were identical."

"That hardly seems life-threatening to me. But tell me, do you at least enjoy the view outside your window?"

"I love it," Lorna said, moving beside him to admire the dark green hills capped with gray clouds, the eucalyptus trees surrounding the courtyard, and the rainbow spray of the fountain. A few students were walking across the courtyard. She checked her watch. "We'd better hurry. Once classes let out we'll never get a table."

As they walked across the campus Lorna remarked, "Most guest lecturers don't stay as long as you're planning to. That's why President Arnold decided to give you the guest cottage. At first he wanted you to stay at his house."

"But not for two weeks."

"He thought you'd need more privacy than that," she replied with conscious tact. "Of course, I usually just book people into the local motels," she added, her thoughts reverting for an instant to the Woebegone Werewolves. Any motel she used for them probably would not accept further college business. She'd have to be very careful.

The coffee house was airy and light, hanging Boston ferns and piggyback plants the only devices used to divide the space between the clean wooden tables. They ordered coffee and croissants from a tanned blond waiter, and Jason smiled. "You know, you could blindfold an Easterner, secretly transport him to any place in Califor-

18

nia, and the minute you took off his blindfold I think he'd know what state he was in."

"Do you say that because of the menu?"

"Well, the avocado and alfalfa sprout sandwiches are a clue, certainly, but not the only one. The real giveaway is the sun. It always shines here, and even if by chance it's not shining, you can see that everyone expects it imminently."

"I can see you've never been here during the rainy season."

"I'm not sure I believe in it at all. Am I keeping you away from your work?" he asked quickly as she glanced at her watch.

"I'm more worried about keeping to your schedule," she told him. "My work can wait."

"Yours must be a very interesting job, if I understand it correctly."

Lorna nodded as she took the last bite of her croissant. "I have a chance to meet a wide variety of people. But not many poets."

"Are you a poetry reader?"

"You could say so." She stirred her coffee unnecessarily, regretting intensely that she hadn't tried harder to get a copy of his book. "I love Auden." She waved her spoon at him, struck by a sudden thought. "It just occurred to me, there's quite a precedent of lawyers being poets. Wallace Stevens, and wasn't Archibald MacLeish a lawyer also?"

"Yes, he went to Harvard Law School but later gave up his law partnership to write poetry. I've consoled myself at times with the thought that I'm in good company. But I'd give a great deal to be able to write like Auden, who was never a lawyer. I'd think you were a little young to appreciate him."

"Well, depending on the definition, I'm either rapidly

19

approaching middle age or I've already arrived," Lorna replied. Her youthful appearance was more often a drawback than an asset in her work, so she was accustomed to announcing, and sometimes exaggerating, her thirty-one years.

"I never imagined I'd meet a fellow Auden fan here, much less a sexy one with such a beautiful nose."

"I must admit, no one's ever said that to me before."

He looked at her appraisingly. "That you're sexy or that you have a beautiful nose?" When she didn't respond, he went on. "I suppose I could have complimented you on your eyes, your hair, your body. But as a poet I feel obliged to be a little more original." His eyes locked with hers and she felt a shock that was almost physical, as if the visual contact had created an electric connection between them.

He must have practiced this technique many times before, but even acknowledging that possibility, she was reluctant to break the spell. "We'd better get your bags and get you settled," she said finally. "You're having lunch with President Arnold in less than an hour. Let me pay the check—it can be my apology for your unnerving experience this morning."

He nodded. As she stood at the cash register she thought that it was nice to be with a man so confident in his masculinity that he didn't need to make an issue of such minor details.

When they stepped out into the bright sunlight he removed his tie and threw his sport coat over his shoulder. Against her will, her eyes were drawn to the now open neck of his shirt, which revealed a few dark curly hairs. He was very slim, his stomach perfectly flat. Seeing him look around with interest, she tried to view the campus through his eyes. The newer concrete and glass structures contrasted strangely with the few older Victorian-style buildings that still housed some of the smaller departments. The fountains, palm trees, and tanned students lent a resortlike flavor to the rather uninspiring architectural mix. And overhead, the sun shone fiercely in a typically blue sky. No wonder he thought it never rained here.

They transferred his leather suitcase from Susan's car to the back of Lorna's green Toyota and she drove him to the cottage, a small adobe building almost hidden by a huge oleander hedge. She parked her car at the edge of the quiet street and led him up the ragged flagstone walk to the front door.

"I've left maps and schedules of your lectures and whatnot right on the coffee table," she told him as she handed him the keys. "The bar and the kitchen have the basic supplies, and I'll be in touch with you later to see if you need anything. You have a very hectic schedule, and today is the worst."

They were still standing awkwardly on the front step of the cottage, Lorna feeling a little reluctant to find herself alone in the cottage with him.

"Are you coming to the events tonight?"

She automatically returned his smile. "Of course!"

"Good." His eyes met hers and again she felt his appeal. Her skin prickled and her face grew warm. Apparently he was an expert at turning on a kind of sexual force whenever he wanted to. Feeling vaguely as if she were making a cowardly retreat, Lorna wished him a pleasant lunch and left. If she was to have time to change clothes before the reading and dinner, she'd have to get right back to her office—there was still a whole fall schedule of chamber music to set up. Lorna vowed to put this dangerously attractive man out of her mind . . . for the time being.

CHAPTER TWO

"I'm Annie." The blue-jeaned young brunette sitting at Susan's desk put down her tattered paperback as Lorna approached. "I came right over because I heard Jason Coulter was arriving this morning."

"You just missed him." Lorna frowned. "Is that the only reason you're here?" It would hardly do to have her office besieged with students hoping for a glimpse of the famous poet.

Annie laughed. "No, I'm your temporary secretary. But I just happen to have three copies of Jason Coulter's book here in my backpack, and I'm hoping to get his autograph."

"Three copies! I couldn't find one in the bookstore, and the library copy is missing. Can you let me borrow one until tomorrow?"

"Sure. This is my copy—the others belong to my roommates. We're all Jason Coulter groupies."

"You're a life saver. This is the first time I've invited someone to speak here without having read his work. A group of students requested him, he had a lot of favorable reviews, so I just went ahead. Now I wish I'd spent more time looking for his book."

"You'll love it," Annie assured her.

"I hope so," Lorna murmured. "Let me show you around and get you started. Then I'll need to write some letters before I go home to change for the reading and the dean's dinner."

Driving home after several hours that had been divided equally between explanations of Annie's work and Annie's rhapsodies about Jason Coulter, Lorna welcomed the familiar hairpin turn onto the winding tree-lined road that led to her house in the hills. The twenty-minute drive home, primarily over lightly traveled roads, provided a breathing space between the hectic atmosphere of work and the more relaxed atmosphere of her small, secluded house. She drove almost unconsciously, automatically adjusting her speed to every dip and curve in the road. The car moved smoothly through tree-shrouded dimness into bright sunlight.

A hawk circled high overhead as she turned the key to her wide front door, and she stopped to admire his flight, shading her eyes with her hand. The living room was cool now that the sun was behind the trees, and she thought once again how much she enjoyed its color scheme of muted blues and cream. She had bought the house after her divorce, using her half of the proceeds from the sale of the large suburban tract house she had shared with her husband. This cottage, nestled among the trees, was a source of great comfort and pride to her. Kicking off her shoes, she turned on the stereo and relaxed on the Oriental-print sofa.

The sun was shining through the oak leaves, creating a kaleidoscope of light and shadow on the cream-colored wall opposite her. The soft music she had selected washed over her as her eyes followed the shapes of the swaying branches. In her mind she heard Jason's voice

23

repeating *Your eyes, your hair, your body,* and she felt a responsive heaviness in her breasts and thighs.

"Time for a cold shower," she said aloud, giving the sofa cushion a vigorous slap as she stood up. This day-dreaming would lead to no good, she knew. Jason Coulter had had an unexpectedly powerful effect on her, one she would do her best to resist during his two-week visit.

After her shower, Lorna dried her hair, then selected from her closet a blue knit dress that would be perfect for the evening's events. The color set off her tan and accented her eyes, and the clingy fabric made the most of her figure. Jason would have no trouble spotting her at the reading, she thought, and frowned at herself in the mirror.

She arrived at the auditorium early to make sure everything was in order. Satisfied, she took a program, selected a good seat, and settled in to wait for the reading. The titles of Jason's poems were intriguing. She took from her purse the slender volume Annie had loaned her and began to read, matching the poems she read to the program for the evening. He was good, better than she had expected. The work could almost be divided into two groups—a set of cynical, rather dry poems about human society, and a smaller set of lyrical poems celebrating nature. Each poem had a date, and upon closer study she decided that he had moved from a bitter, hostile position toward a more positive one. Several poems listed on the program were too recent to have appeared in the book, and she wondered what their mood would be.

Once the program got under way, Lorna shut out all distractions and concentrated on the warm, deep voice. Jason read steadily for an hour, then took a short break. When he left the stage Lorna felt as if she were waking from a trance. His poems, read in that powerful voice, had touched a core in her memory, evoking times and

24

emotions she had buried and thought forgotten. There was pain in his poetry that deepened the lines in his face as he read and caused Lorna to dig her nails into her palms. But there was healing, too, and rejoicing, and an ease in being alive that Lorna knew she had not yet found. Perhaps Jason had an ability to tap universal human experiences, but it seemed more as if he and Lorna held something unique in common.

After a brief intermission, the audience listened respectfully as Jason answered questions. He good-naturedly explained what lawyers and poets had in common (words), why he didn't write in blank verse (too hard), and why he didn't answer personal questions. He would be a great teacher, Lorna thought. He had a good rapport with students, but easily maintained his authority. He was witty. He was charming. And he had the most captivating blue eyes she'd ever seen.

The dinner was a large one, and even the dean's big, high-ceilinged living room seemed crowded as the last guests arrived for cocktails. Lorna's face was quickly flushed from her single glass of wine and from the praise she'd been receiving for getting Jason to the college. The guest of honor was backed into a corner across the room, surrounded by admirers and looking pleased but slightly disheveled.

"They'll eat him alive if he's not careful," a professor's wife remarked to Lorna with a grin. "And I can hardly blame them. He must have some flaw, but I can't imagine what it is."

Lorna nodded absently. Jason Coulter was a hero to one and all. She wanted to tell him how much she had enjoyed the reading, but not at the expense of elbowing other fans aside.

The dinner was pleasant, and Lorna enjoyed her seat

next to an elderly professor of medieval history. He was a notorious eccentric and never restrained his acid comments about fellow faculty members. Tonight he was in fine form, describing the new dean of administration. Lorna had never met the man, but judging from the laughter from nearby diners, the professor's remarks were apt. "A true believer in rules and regulations. He's never once struck a match without first closing the matchbook cover."

As the dinner guests moved to the living room to sip liqueur, Jason suddenly appeared at Lorna's side.

"Susan's car safely at home?"

"Oh, no, I forgot all about it. And I promised Dale I'd have it back tonight."

"You'll need another car. Why don't you let me help you if you're here alone. I'll drive Susan's car and then you can drive me home in your car."

"You must be tired after such a long day. I'd better get someone else."

"Nonsense." His voice was husky from the reading. "If you refuse my help, I'll think you're afraid to be alone with me."

"That's ridiculous. I was simply trying to be considerate." Lorna responded quickly before she realized he was joking.

He laughed softly and she smiled. "All right. If you feel you must drive Susan's car, I'll be grateful for your help." She wished she could sound a little more gracious, but the prospect of being alone with him did make her feel tense.

"I really enjoyed your poems," Lorna chattered as soon as they had said their good-byes and left. "I saw a review that compared you to Dylan Thomas, but you're less romantic, it seems to me." She was talking too much

26

and too rapidly, and his amused look told her he was well aware of the cause.

"You're more like Auden, with a little Robert Frost mixed in," she hurried on as they approached the parking lot. She gave him the keys, carefully avoiding his eyes. "Follow me. It's only a few miles."

Susan's house was brightly lit, and Dale, a graduate student at a nearby university, came out when he heard the car. "It's a boy," he announced, barely waiting for the introductions to be complete. "And in honor of the occasion, we've named him Jason." He grinned at Jason.

"I'm flattered," the poet replied.

"Well, we owe you a lot," Dale said.

"Not really. After all, anyone can drive a car. If I'd had to deliver the baby, that would have been different."

"Susan would love for you to visit her, if you would," Dale said. "She loves your work, and she also wants to thank you for being so understanding this morning."

Jason hesitated. "I'd enjoy seeing my namesake and chatting with your wife when she's a little more relaxed than she was this morning, but I don't have a car here." He thought for a moment. "I have tomorrow morning free, and I can probably arrange to rent a car."

"I'll drive you over tomorrow and we can visit together," Lorna said. If he was going to be nice enough to make the requested visit, at least he shouldn't have to go to any more trouble than necessary.

"Susan will be thrilled." Dale looked at his watch. "I've got to get back in the house and finish making my phone calls."

"It's nice of you to go to see Susan," Lorna remarked as she drove back to Jason's cottage, very aware of him beside her in the dark interior of the car. "I know how busy you are here."

"Tomorrow was left relatively free to give me some

time to recover from today. And if I were to be completely honest, I almost enjoyed my experience this morning." He turned toward her and she glanced away from the road, but his face was shadowed and unreadable. "Perhaps we can have lunch afterward."

Lorna hesitated briefly, then rebelled against her own timidity. "That would be nice." Her tone was satisfyingly cool.

She had never met a man quite like Jason. His promise to visit Susan showed a sensitivity and thoughtfulness that Lorna never would have expected from anyone so successful, even a successful poet. No doubt his behavior toward her would be more predictable. In her work she had met a number of famous and not so famous men who expected to find sexual gratification on every campus they visited, and who assumed that Lorna was there to provide it. Probably the only difference in Jason Coulter was that in his case she found herself almost tempted to prove the assumption correct. His hand touched her shoulder lightly and she jumped as if he had hit an exposed nerve.

"Would you fall into a maidenly faint if I asked you in for some coffee?" Lorna grimaced as he went on. "I have some questions about my schedule that I'd like to clear up."

The invitation was not unexpected, although she had still maintained some hope that he was not the typical male celebrity. In any case, he had left her little choice. "I'd be glad to help."

His fingers brushed lightly across her back as she stood beside him in front of the hedge, and she preceded him carefully up the dark walk, still feeling the warm trail of his touch on her shoulder. The cottage was completely dark inside, and her stomach tightened as the door clicked shut behind them. Jason led her with him to a

28

nearby lamp, his hand closing gently on her bare arm, and the contact contributed to her tension.

She sat down carefully at one end of the beige tweed sofa, gnawing on a thumbnail as Jason disappeared into the kitchen. The sound of his returning footsteps made her lick her lips nervously.

Jason poured two cups of coffee, handed her one, and sat down at the other end of the sofa.

She raised her cup to her lips, suddenly uncertain how to make conversation.

"Are you married?" he asked, and she looked at him quickly, surprised he wouldn't have noticed her ringless fingers.

"Well, it just seemed a little more polite than confirming that you're single," he explained, "and I would like to know."

Without embellishing, she informed him that she was divorced.

"I'm divorced also," he said, "but it was so long ago it could have happened to someone else. I'm used to being alone."

"Doesn't it get lonely, off by yourself in Vermont?"

"You can't be terribly lonely unless you're lonely for a specific person, I think. I have an elderly couple living on the property to help me take care of the place, so I'm not completely isolated. And, contrary to popular belief, I'm not holed up there all the time."

"It must have been a big change for you after New York City."

"Yes, and a change was just what I needed. I'd had a surfeit of high finance, liquor, and expensive cars. For years I'd been denying something that was an important part of me."

She leaned forward, intrigued, and he made a sweeping motion with one hand, as if to brush away what he'd said. "I won't go into all of that—I always knew what I was doing, and why, but gradually I saw that my reasons were no longer valid, if they ever had been." His gaze seemed to turn inward, focusing on some private knowledge that tautened his face and deepened the shadows under his eyes and below his cheekbones.

She felt like an intruder, watching his pain, and decided to introduce a more neutral topic.

"Did you plan to write poetry when you first went to Vermont?"

"I hoped to write something, probably the great American novel, but poetry is what happened."

She smiled a little, twisting her cup around in the saucer. "It's surprising to meet you, to find that you're so human. I'd expect a poet to be withdrawn, moody, something along those lines."

"I suppose Vermont serves that purpose for me. When I'm on one of my brief forays into the world, I enjoy human contact, particularly with an attractive woman like you." He looked at her expectantly, but she ignored the flattery.

"You had some questions?"

"Of course." He gave her another look, then produced a copy of the schedule from the bookshelf beside the sofa. He sat down next to her, so close that their thighs touched. Lorna shifted uneasily, aware of the warmth of his leg through her knit dress as they leafed through the typewritten pages. Each time he pointed out a line, his arm brushed across hers, occasionally making fleeting contact with her breasts. She felt helpless, trapped against the arm of the sofa and somehow too timid simply to stand up and walk away from his subtle tortures. All her senses seemed centered on the side of her body that pressed against him, and her thoughts were scattered, impossible to focus on his questions.

Finally he put the papers down and turned back to her, one arm resting lightly across her shoulders.

"You know," she said awkwardly, "I read your poems for the first time just a few hours ago."

"Did you like them?"

He seemed honestly to care about her opinion, and she answered shyly, aware that he was used to adulation. "They were wonderful. Some were particularly meaningful to me."

He was looking directly into her eyes, and their faces seemed very close together. "Which ones?"

Lorna shook her head. "It seems too self-revealing somehow. We're barely acquainted, but if I named the poems that spoke to me, you'd know me better than my closest friend."

He laughed, pulling away from her to throw his head back against the sofa. "Has it occurred to you that in writing those poems I exposed my innermost thoughts to anyone with a library card or a few dollars? Surely I can ask you to reciprocate."

"Perhaps you're more of an exhibitionist than I am. I couldn't bear the thought of complete strangers knowing so much about me."

"Well, I'm not going to stand on my rights as a poet, although someday I would like to hear what you found in my work."

Someday? He would be in California for only two weeks.

"I'm glad we'll be having lunch tomorrow," he said. "When I came into your office today, before you knew I was there, I was reminded of Sleeping Beauty, and for a moment I was tempted to try out the role of the handsome prince."

She moved away a few inches, and he reached over to take her hand. "Don't be afraid of me. I admit I'm attracted to you, but I'm not trying to rush you into anything."

"I'm not afraid." To prove the point, she let her icy fingers lie stiffly in his warm hand. "I value my independence, and I'm not interested in a romantic relationship."

"What kind of relationship interests you?"

"Friendship," she said, annoyed to hear that the word had come out sounding like a question rather than a firm statement of principle.

"Friendship," he echoed with a smile. "That's as good a starting place as any, I suppose."

"A starting and ending place. I don't want a serious relationship or a brief, meaningless affair. But I do think I'd like to be friends with you. Very much," she added shyly, disturbed by his serious expression.

"Don't ask me for a guarantee that I won't try to change your mind," he said finally. She bit her lip, and he let go of her hand to gesture warningly. "But for now we'll leave it at that."

She stood up and moved to the door, her fingers clenched into the soft leather of her purse.

"Good night, Lorna. Don't forget to pick me up in the morning." The intensity of his sparkling blue eyes set her heart racing. Quickly she turned away, ducking her head a little, and called "Good night" without looking back.

Once home, she undressed quickly and fell into bed, but sleep was elusive. She should stay away from Jason Coulter, she told herself. But now, alone in her bed, she remembered the pressure of his thigh against hers, the tantalizing sensation of his arm brushing her breasts, and she moved restlessly under the sheets. Tonight she had been protected by his sensitivity to her fears. But she couldn't deny her vulnerability to him if he refused to accept the limits she had tried to place on their relationship.

She woke up feeling groggy and deliberately dressed in what she privately considered her least attractive outfit— a straight navy blue skirt and a tailored white blouse. A touch of pink lip gloss was her only concession to femininity, and as she looked in the mirror at her shadowed eyes and pale cheeks, she had a momentary fear that her effort to look unappealing might be too successful. At least she would have a chance to change before her date with Brian. She certainly needed no protection against him, and it would be unfair to turn up looking like someone's maiden aunt.

After getting Annie started on a series of letters to potential guest speakers for an American history lecture series, she sat in on a drama department meeting about establishing an actor- or actress-in-residence program. Then, with the rest of the morning free, she drove directly to Jason's cottage.

He greeted her with a half smile, seeming to speculate on her rather prim appearance. He himself was dressed in gray slacks and a plaid sport shirt that revealed the dusting of sunbleached hair on his forearms.

"Will an autographed copy of my book be an adequate gift, do you think?"

Lorna nodded as they got into the car. "She'll love it, but your visit will be the most valuable gift. It's a very nice thing to do."

"Actually, I'm grateful for my experience with her yesterday. It made me feel a part of the human community somehow. How long have you been divorced?"

Startled by the apparent non sequitur, she replied automatically, "A little over a year, I guess."

"That's not too long ago. I admit it took me almost eighteen years to get over my marriage, but I always was a slow learner."

Lorna didn't answer, concentrating now on finding a

free space in the hospital parking lot. As she pulled triumphantly into a newly vacant space marked Staff Only, Jason said, "You know, I'm really torn between renting my own car and having you at my beck and call, but I think after lunch I'll ask you to drop me off at a rental agency. I never thought of myself as the typical American male, but I must say I've found not having a car somewhat emasculating."

She looked at him briefly. "I hadn't noticed." At his grin, she went on. "I wish the college could afford to supply you with transportation, but the money's just not there. And most guests are here so briefly. . . ."

Susan, as Lorna expected, looked beautiful. According to the whispered aside of one nurse, half the morning had been devoted to preparing for Jason's visit. Next to the brunette's bright flowered bed jacket and glowing smile, Lorna felt dowdy and morose. Jason was impressive, charming to Susan and her roommate and properly admiring of the small pink baby. His gift was very well received, as was Lorna's of a tiny hand-crocheted sweater and booties.

"I haven't made anything for the baby yet," Susan confided. "I thought it would give me something to do while I'm sitting around the house taking care of him."

"I doubt you'll find you have too much time on your hands," Lorna remarked, remembering when Beth's children were tiny babies.

"Maybe you're right." Susan's smile grew broader. "Our St. Bernard is expecting a litter of puppies any day."

Lorna concealed her horror until they left. "Susan has always been very devil-may-care, and things usually work out for her, but this time I think she'll have her hands full, with a baby and puppies too. Who knows, though, for her it may all go as smoothly as she expects. How many women could look so gorgeous the day after giving birth?"

"Not many, I expect, but I'm hardly an expert. And even in your prison warden's uniform, you look more beautiful than she."

Warmed despite herself by the compliment, Lorna offered him the car keys.

"Is this a concession to my masculine ego?"

Lorna shrugged. "I guess I was trying to assuage my guilt over not renting you a car."

He took the keys and opened the passenger door for her. "This way I can be sure you'll keep our date for lunch. If I let you drive, you'd probably rush back to the campus and barricade yourself in your office."

The Mexican restaurant Jason had chosen for lunch on a friend's recommendation was not far from the campus. It was unostentatious, created from an old wood-frame house. Meals were served in several rooms, each of which contained in addition to several dining tables a few overstuffed chairs and shelves lined with old leatherbound books. Lorna and Jason were seated next to a window overlooking a courtyard overgrown with mint and golden poppies. On the far side of the window was a mahogany hutch containing a variety of china plates and cups, their once bright patterns faded and soft.

They chatted easily about restaurants and food, and Lorna began to relax the barriers she had erected against involvement. Jason was the most amusing and intelligent man she had ever met. It was impossible for her to resist his charms, and, thank heaven, it was also unnecessary as long as he accepted the role of friend. She was replete and contented, having eaten two spicy chicken enchiladas and drunk half a dark Mexican beer, when Jason said, "I expect to be very busy for a while, catching up with old friends and meeting my commitments here. But I'll call you in a day or two. By then I hope you will have had time to reconsider your position. In principle, at least."

Lorna refused to be drawn into an argument. "I enjoy your company, but it's not going to go further than that. I know what I want out of life."

"And it's not love." He didn't seem particularly downcast, Lorna noted. He just drank his beer with an infuriating air of superior wisdom.

She left him at a nearby car rental office and drove back to the campus. In her job, irregular hours were the rule, since many of the events she arranged took place in the evening or on weekends. As a consequence, she was expected to take time off during the week, and today she was tempted to go home. A long day, a poor night's sleep, and half a beer at lunch had hardly prepared her for an afternoon's work, and she decided to clear her desk and then leave for the day. She could never sleep in the afternoon no matter how much she might like to, but at least she could spend some time outdoors before her date.

Annie had typed half of the letters, but she showed a regrettable tendency to be careless, and several of them had to be retyped. The rest Lorna signed and put out to be mailed.

There was only a small amount of correspondence in her basket. A memo from the English Department announcing that Jason had agreed to conduct a seminar on modern poetry. An updated calendar from the Music Department—Lorna tried to keep from competing with their recitals. And a memo from the administrative dean whom the elderly professor had joked about the night before at dinner.

"Your college degree has been omitted from your personnel file. Please enter the information in the blanks

36

below so I can update your records," she read. She shrugged, wrote "No degree received," and put the memo back in the campus mail. Then after seeing that Annie had plenty to do, she left.

As she shifted into second gear for the steep driveway up to her house, Lorna noticed several clumps of poison oak growing in the brush. Pulling that out would be her afternoon's activity, she decided. The landscaping for her house was done in what was called a "natural" style, meaning that there was no lawn or flowerbeds to maintain. So she really didn't mind her one gardening chore of keeping the area cleared of poison oak, except for the possibility of accidentally touching the plant. She exchanged her skirt, blouse, and sandals for jeans, a heavy shirt, and hiking boots. Equipped with gardening gloves and a shovel, she worked until late afternoon, when no leaf of poison oak remained.

The hard physical labor had made her feel pleasantly tired, and once her clothes were safely in the washing machine, she decided to treat herself to a bath rather than her usual shower. She added some herb-scented bath oil to the warm water and lay back, sliding down until the water came just to her chin. After relaxing for fifteen minutes in the bath she would be as good as new.

The doorbell rang as she was putting on her lipstick. It was always a pleasure to see Brian, who came up from Los Angeles on business once or twice a month. Lorna had met him a year ago on a flight from Seattle, where she had been attending a conference, and since then they had become good friends. Brian had easily accepted her wish to keep their relationship platonic, so Lorna never felt uncomfortable about being with him. She wore her favorite dress—a silk of muted pastels, and had taken some care with her makeup. Looking so unfeminine during the day had depressed her, but now she felt like herself again, and Brian's admiring glance when she opened the door confirmed her confidence.

It certainly was nice, she thought as she lay in bed later, to spend an evening with a man without feeling constantly on guard. And if dates with Brian or her other male friends seemed flat in comparison to the little time she had spent with Jason Coulter, that was all to the good. A man as compelling as Jason, if she allowed him to come too close, might find it ridiculously easy to dominate her. As she had learned during her marriage, she was much too eager to please the man she loved, even at the expense of her own identity. Not that she was in love with Jason, of course. But she couldn't deny that she found him unusually attractive.

Through her success at work she had gained a measure of self-esteem, but her strength had never been tested in an intimate relationship. Somehow she suspected that even a two-week affair with such a powerful, self-assured man would turn her back into a clinging, dependent rag doll. She'd have to be very careful to protect herself, she decided as she drifted off to sleep.

The next several days passed rather uneventfully—Susan made a brief visit to the office to show off her baby, the Woebegone Werewolves made it known that they could not possibly appear at Crowley for less than twice the agreed-upon fee, and Beth called to ask Lorna about a rumor that she had been seeing Jason Coulter. Lorna was annoyed by Beth's call, unreasonably so, since she was able to say quite truthfully that she had not spoken to Jason for three days. Beth, who seemed unusually enthusiastic about the rumored relationship, obstinately refused to take Lorna's disavowal seriously.

"But you have been out with him."

"We've gone on a few errands together, true. Nothing

that could be called a date. And anyway, who's keeping you informed?"

Infuriatingly, Beth had ignored her question. "Don't worry, dear. I'm sure he'll be in touch with you soon."

Lorna's reply was sharp. "Don't be silly. If I actually wanted to see the man again, I wouldn't hesitate to call him myself."

Beth's horrified gasp restored her to good humor, however, and they ended the conversation on a happier note as Lorna laughed. "Relax. I have no intention of pursuing him."

Despite her protestations, Lorna was uncomfortably aware of the time that had elapsed since Jason had told her he would call in a day or two, and she rather enjoyed the opportunity to enter into fierce negotiations with the Werewolves' manager. To his protests that their new hit album would make them worth considerably more than her original offer, she countered with assurances that by the time the concert took place the Werewolves' popularity would no doubt have declined to the point where it would be difficult to sell tickets at any but bargain prices. Furthermore, she pointed out, their so-called hit was not even on the charts, and probably never would be unless they had more public exposure.

On Saturday morning Lorna was not surprised to receive a tearful telephone call from Susan. "The vet says Brandy's going to have at least five puppies any minute now, and I just don't know what I'm going to do. The baby cries all night and if I have to listen to a bunch of puppies yipping and whimpering, I think I'll die."

"How would it be," Lorna said, "if I came by and got Brandy and brought her up here for a few weeks until you've got things under control?"

Susan sniffed. "Oh, Lorna, would you? I'd be so grateful. It would only be for a week, actually. Then Dale's brother will be back from his vacation and he'll keep her for us."

"I have a tennis game this afternoon, and I'll stop by around five—if you think she'll fit in my car."

"We'll shove her in somehow," Susan assured her, and after a few comforting remarks about the baby, Lorna went back to her vacuuming.

Already she was regretting her impulsive offer. Brandy had been an enormous dog when Lorna had last seen her, and she hadn't even been pregnant then. She'd need some enclosed space in the yard for the daytime, and maybe she'd consent to sleep in the garage at night. Or on the deck. With a sigh Lorna went out to the garage and pulled down the stairs to the loft. As she had remembered, there was a huge roll of wire fencing and several crates she could use to make a place for Brandy and her puppies, should they arrive. She spent the rest of the morning on the project and by lunchtime was quite happy with the small dog run she had created near the deck, using several handy trees to help support the fencing. After a quick lunch of cottage cheese and pineapple she changed into her tennis shorts and left.

She returned home at dinnertime, tired and hungry, her car loaded down with dog, dogfood, and dog blankets. Brandy seemed confused, but amiably so, and settled down to a healthy dinner in her run while Lorna poured herself a glass of wine.

"Another big night on the town for us," she remarked to Brandy as she sat on the deck. "I don't know how much longer I can keep up the pace." She had nothing scheduled for Sunday, and it promised to be a long day. She was considering calling Beth and wangling an invitation to dinner without any eligible male being included when the telephone rang.

Beth, Lorna decided as she ran lightly into the kitchen. *And for once I'll be properly grateful.*

"Lorna?"

Her heart thumped once very hard at the sound of the unexpected baritone voice, and she scowled at her faint reflection in the kitchen window.

"Hi, Jason. How are you?"

"Fine. I'm in Carmel for the weekend, but I plan to be back tomorrow afternoon and I'd like to take you to dinner if you're free."

Lorna jumped at the chance to escape the solitary evening she had pictured.

"I'd love to have dinner."

"Good. I'm not completely sure what time I'll be back, so I'll call you from the cottage and we can agree on a time. Have you missed me?"

Lorna laughed. "I didn't even know you were gone."

Jason's voice rang confidently in her ear. "Sooner or later you'll change your tune."

"Don't count on it," Lorna replied cheerfully, and hung up. It might be foolish to spend any more time with Jason, but it was impossible to refuse the opportunity to see him again. As long as she was careful, she could have her cake and nibble at the frosting too.

CHAPTER THREE

Lorna awoke on Sunday with a vague feeling of anticipation that at first she could not pin down. As she realized it was her dinner with Jason—not the presence of Brandy or the prospect of a day off—that had elevated her mood, she felt a little disturbed. Had she already become dependent on the man? The evidence was there, since she had been depressed and irritable before his call and quite the reverse afterward. It was fine to enjoy being with him, but not to the point where his presence or absence controlled her moods.

There weren't yet any puppies in the garage, and Brandy seemed to be in good spirits, so Lorna put on a sweater and took the dog out for a pre-breakfast stroll. The low morning clouds had not yet burned off, and they encountered no traffic on the road. Lorna picked up her Sunday paper from the group of mailboxes at the bottom of the hill, then took a rapidly tiring Brandy home for a mountainous breakfast of dogfood.

She had almost finished reading the newspaper when she noticed that Brandy seemed to be trying to get out of her run. With a shrug she took the panting dog into the kitchen and showed her the refrigerator carton she had lined with old towels. Brandy stepped through the windowlike opening and disappeared into the dark interior of the box. Uncertain of the next step, Lorna sat down at her kitchen table, idly checking the group of cacti on the windowsill for any new growth. All was silent in the box, and she began to swing one leg nervously. Eventually she got a flashlight from the garage and peered carefully at Brandy, who stared back impassively. Feeling increasingly useless, Lorna vainly offered a dish of water, then washed her breakfast dishes and fixed herself a bacon and avocado sandwich for lunch.

"A watched pot never boils," she murmured. Her hovering probably made Brandy nervous. Valiantly resisting the temptation to peek into the box again, she wandered impatiently through the house. She could hardly go off and leave the poor thing if Brandy really was ready to have her puppies, but Lorna's chores were done and she rebelled at the prospect of spending such a beautiful afternoon at home. With a sense of unappreciated virtue, she took a book out and sat under a tree. But she found herself thinking more about the dog than about what she was reading. By the time Jason called at five she was ready to scream from boredom, and the knowledge that she would have to cancel their date did not improve her humor.

"I don't know how to tell you this, but I have Susan's dog and I think she's about to have her puppies. I just can't leave her."

Jason laughed. "That's a novel excuse, anyway. Given the effect I have on her household, Susan should be glad I don't visit California more often."

"Sheer coincidence, I'm sure. But I'm sorry about our dinner."

"All need not be lost. Tell me how to get to your house, and I'll pick up something for dinner and bring it over."

"You mean you expect me to cook?" Lorna demanded. "Or are you planning to play chef?"

"Would it win your heart if I cooked dinner?"

Lorna hesitated. "No, but it would make a good impression."

"That's not enough. I hate cooking in other people's kitchens anyway. I'll impress you with my culinary skills another time. For tonight I'll get something already prepared."

Lorna provided him with detailed directions to her house, then contemplated her worn jeans and faded cotton shirt. Appropriate for taking care of a pregnant dog, perhaps, but surely she could come up with something a little nicer to wear for Jason. Upstairs in her bedroom, she finally laid out a pair of white cotton slacks and a pale blue cotton sweater. After showering and washing her hair, she put on her laciest, most feminine bikini panties and bra, deliberately refusing to consider her reasons for doing so. After all, she had bought the expensive underwear on a ridiculous impulse, and she had to wear it sometime.

Interrupted only by a quick trip down to the kitchen to discover that Brandy's condition hadn't changed, she dried her hair and dressed. A pale lipstick, a few touches of perfume at her throat and wrists, and she was ready. Pacing her living room, she found her attention more scattered than it had been all day, her mind veering between the driveway and the kitchen with every imagined noise. Hoping to quiet her tingling nerves, she put a light jazz record on the stereo and poured herself a small glass of white wine.

The sound of a car in the driveway came as she was turning the record over, and she hurried out to help Jason carry whatever food he had brought. She inhaled sharply when she saw him, a tingle running up and down

44

her spine. He was dressed casually in tan slacks and a striped sport shirt. He'd gotten some sun at the beach, and his nose was faintly sunburned.

"Potato salad, green olives, and beer," he announced. When he smiled, the whiteness of his teeth gleamed against his new tan. "Baklava for dessert. And for my real surprise, chicken à la W. H. Auden."

It took her a few seconds to remember the story about Auden. On his way to a dinner party he had accidentally run over a chicken in the road, and presented the still warm corpse to his hostess to cook for dinner. Lorna blanched at the thought.

"You didn't—there are no chickens around here," she protested as he produced a paper bag.

"And I thought you loved Auden." Jason shook his head.

"His poetry, not his idiosyncrasies. Rather, I enjoy reading about them, not meeting them in the flesh."

"No pun intended? Relax. This chicken is barbecued." He carried the food into the house and stacked it neatly on the kitchen counter.

"And this is the famous dog," he commented, peering into the carton with the flashlight. "Not exactly a beehive of activity in there, is it?"

"No, and I'm getting worried," Lorna said. "How can I tell if something's wrong?"

"I think she'd let you know." After opening a few cupboards he found some tall beer glasses and poured out a bottle for himself. "To us."

Lorna silently clinked her wineglass to his and led him out to the deck. He seemed to feel right at home. If she left him in the kitchen much longer, he'd probably start reorganizing the cabinets.

"I had no idea country living was so close by. I even

saw several stables on my way out here," he said, looking out at the trees.

"This is horse country," Lorna agreed, fighting an urge to gnaw on her fingernails. Unable to think of a topic for conversation, she listened gratefully while Jason went on to describe his newfound fondness for rural life. The slightest movement of his hands as he spoke drew her eyes irresistibly. Each time he took a sip of beer she followed the motion to his mouth as if she were hypnotized. She felt hypersensitive to the faint sounds of the breeze in the trees, to the rise and fall of his voice. She responded almost breathlessly to his remarks, feeling the heat rise in her cheeks.

"You almost seem to have the best of both worlds here," he concluded. "A quiet country house not too far from your work."

"Well," Lorna hedged, "there are actually a lot of houses around, hidden in the trees. When the dogs start barking, or someone gets out the chain saw, it seems more suburban. But it does provide a wonderful break from my job."

"I'm rather interested in your job. How does one qualify for such a variety of activities?"

"I worked my way into it. About three years ago I started at Crowley in a part-time job helping to arrange conferences on the campus. Gradually they consolidated different functions into the one job, and now I handle the majority of conferences and guest appearances. But it came about slowly, so I had plenty of time to learn my way."

"And have there been no men in your life since your divorce?"

"I have friends who are men, but I suppose that's not what you're asking."

"No, I just wondered if perhaps you were recovering from a recent unhappy love affair."

She laughed. "No, thank goodness."

He looked at her steadily over the rim of his glass. "I can tell you from my own experience—if you continue to shut men out of your life, you'll regret it later."

"I doubt it, but if you're right, then I'll just have to face that problem when it arises." She stood up abruptly. "I'll put the dinner on the plates."

"Mind if I look around?" He began to prowl the house without waiting for her reply, and Lorna shook her head with a small smile as she heard a board creak upstairs. She would hardly be surprised to find him taking a short nap in the bedroom before dinner. At least he hadn't turned on the television. As she set the redwood picnic table with a checked tablecloth and napkins, she heard another record begin and his voice behind her.

"You have a very eclectic record collection. Many of the musicians I've never even heard of."

"That's been one of the nice things about my job. I've been exposed to a wide variety of music and literature, and I've enjoyed it all. Well, most of it," she amended, thinking of the Woebegone Werewolves.

He nodded. "After I began trying to write poetry I started reading other poets, and I was pleasantly surprised. Poets aren't widely appreciated in this country, but despite that there's a great deal of very good poetry being written here. Incidentally," he went on with a lightning change of topic that momentarily disconcerted her, "what is the purpose of all those fierce plants up there on the windowsill? Are they supposed to discourage burglars?"

Lorna laughed. "That's my cactus garden. Someone gave me a little souvenir cactus a few years ago, a lace cactus, and one day it got a great big flower on it and

47

looked pretty exotic. So I got interested and started getting cuts of other kinds, a bishop's cap and a pincushion. They don't need much care, and when they bloom it's rather exciting."

"The friends I visited in Carmel had a rock garden—I didn't like that either. I prefer either a flower garden or if it's necessary to have something ugly, a vegetable garden. At least that way you can eat the vegetables."

Lorna sighed dramatically. "Since you provided the dinner, I suppose you can be as insulting as you choose. Still, the well-mannered guest . . ."

". . . does not criticize the hostess," Jason concluded with a wry smile. "Perhaps I can make up for my offensive remarks about your plants by saying that you look lovely tonight, and I really like your taste in houses. Also you smell nice and I'm glad to be here."

"Thank you," Lorna said with a broad smile, feeling almost indecently happy. She inspected the table and found nothing missing.

"Surely you don't intend to drink white wine with barbecued chicken?" he asked as they sat down. "You need something that won't be overpowered, like beer."

"This is cheap wine," she assured him. "Nothing could overpower it. You beer drinkers think beer goes with everything."

"You may be right, but I'm going to get another beer. Can I get you anything?"

A few moments later he called softly from the sliding door, "Lorna! There's a puppy in the box."

She nearly spilled her wine in her rush to look at the small, damp puppy nuzzling blindly up to his mother.

"She seems to have everything under control," Jason said softly as they watched together. "I think you can stop worrying."

"Well, she's got at least four more coming," Lorna reminded him. "But I do feel much better about the whole thing. We probably should leave her alone."

By the time they had finished eating, the sun was almost behind the trees and the air had grown cool. Jason put his arm around her and she slid closer to him along the bench, warming herself against his body. His fingers moved softly up and down her forearm, which was bare, since she had pushed up the sleeves of her sweater. The crickets were chirping rhythmically, and Lorna felt an overpowering sense of inertia, as if she could always stay just as she was. When the last rays of light had disappeared she said softly, "This reminds me of a phrase I really liked in one of your poems. 'The soft apologies of crickets.' "

"Yes, I was rather proud of that, although it's not my best poem by any means." His voice, too, was hushed, as if they were conspiring together.

"Another line that really struck me was about the little girl 'with hair that flies like feathers from the nest.' That reminded me so much of my niece when she was very small. It must be marvelous to be able to create such striking images with just a few words."

Jason laughed softly. "I could sit here and let you flatter me all night, but I think perhaps we should move inside. It's getting chilly, and as much as I enjoy having you next to me, I have to admit my arm is getting stiff."

Lorna laughed and moved away regretfully, smoothing down her hair. "I'll make coffee to go with the baklava."

She couldn't resist another peek into the box, and this time there were two puppies, the new one a darker shade of brown.

"Just the same," she remarked as she brought in a tray with the honey-nut pastries and coffee, "I'll be glad when Susan's brother-in-law can take over the dog-sitting. If

49

I'd wanted six St. Bernards, I would have gotten them long before this."

She sat down awkwardly next to Jason on the sofa and poured the coffee. He had turned the lights on, and she was grateful that he had not created a standard seduction scene—soft music and a darkened room. She recognized with a small thrill that this was the moment she had been both dreading and anticipating since they had agreed to have dinner at her house. He watched her solemnly, as if he could read the anxieties in her face.

"I wonder how many calories there are in this," she said as she bit delicately into her baklava.

"About the equivalent of half a jar of honey, I guess. It's no good trying to be so dainty. They're hopelessly messy. And now you've got honey all over your face and fingers."

Lorna reached for a napkin. "And you haven't even tried yours."

"I had my reasons," Jason said, moving the napkins out of reach and taking her hand by the wrist. "This is how I prefer mine." He raised her hand to his mouth and began delicately licking the honey from her fingers. Lorna gave one half-hearted tug to recapture her hand, then succumbed to the intimacy of the moment as his teeth nipped gently at one finger. He patted her hand gently with a napkin, then slipped one arm over her shoulders and smiled.

"Now for your lips." Her heart thudded loudly against her chest as he pushed a strand of hair back from her face and slowly lowered his lips to hers. He brushed her lips lightly, then pulled back for a moment before catching her lower lip carefully between his teeth.

Just for a minute, she promised herself. She wanted only a small portion of an experience which she could not permit herself to complete. There was no reason to reject

50

the sensation of his lips on hers, the heat that seemed to be transmitted from his body to hers. She sighed and moved her hands to his neck as his tongue moved warmly over her lips. Her fingers explored the soft, thick hair at the back of his head as she drew him closer. He sucked softly at her tingling lower lip and gave it several tiny bites until she moaned, twisting her body to press her breasts against his chest.

She felt his heartbeat, heard his breath coming faster, and gloried in the knowledge that he was as aroused as she was. With a long sigh he pushed her back to raise her sweater over her head. He gripped her bare shoulder for an instant, then buried his face in the warm hollow between her breasts, breathing her name before he unhooked her bra and lifted it away from her body. The cool air against her breasts made her excitingly aware of how free she was, how exposed to his eyes, and her nipples were erect and tingling even before he caressed them with his fingers, the circling strokes sending waves of sensation down her body.

"Ever since I first saw you I've wanted to touch you like this, wondered how it would be." Lorna's eyes were closed. She felt dazed, as if she were living out her fantasy, listening to the deep voice saying all the things she had imagined that first day in her office. "I wondered how your breasts would look, how they would feel." He covered her breasts with his hands and she opened her eyes to see him watching her, his pupils dilated with desire. He made a sound deep in his throat and kissed her swollen lips fiercely. His breath was against her cheek then, quick and urgent. "I've been thinking about this all evening."

He pulled her down to lie on her back, her hips across his legs, and he bent to excite her further with his tongue and teeth, nibbling and stroking until she gasped with pleasure. His fingers moved over her neck, her arm, her stomach as his mouth stayed at her breast, and she moaned more loudly, twisting her hips to press hard against him.

She caressed his neck with trembling fingers, then moved quickly to unbutton his shirt. She reached the top buttons easily, then finished the rest as he stretched out beside her, his lips against hers. She ran her hands up his chest, reveling in the prickling sensation of curling hair against her fingers, then slipped her arms around his shoulders, pulling him until their bare skin was touching, her breasts flattened against his chest, both their hearts pounding heavily.

His tongue probed her mouth, exploring the sensitive membranes as his fingers moved urgently over her back. She met his tongue with her own, her hips moving in a demanding rhythm as her need grew. She felt feverish with desire, her blood rushing, skin burning, all of her needing him. She gasped with relief when his hand moved to the waistband of her slacks, his mouth again at her breast.

"Your skin is so soft, so beautiful." His voice was husky, almost choked. "I want to touch all of you."

His hand stroked over the skin of her stomach under her slacks, each time drawing tantalizingly closer to the center of the sensations that were flooding her body. "Please, Jason," she groaned, moving to unbuckle his belt. His hand crept under the lace of her panties, and she was lifting her hips to help him remove them when she was struck by the magnitude of what she was doing. A trickle of fear began to erode her excitement, and she realized that she had let things go much further than she had intended. It was too late to stop now; after all, they weren't teenagers.

But her thoughts had cooled her ardor, and Jason

seemed to sense the change in her as he murmured, "Lorna, tell me you want to make love with me. I want to know all of you. I want to make you mine."

"No." She shook her head miserably, then sat up and moved away from him, pulling her sweater back on. His words had been the catalyst that solidified her vague feelings of unease. "I won't belong to any man. I was a possession once, and I learned the hard way that I couldn't survive that kind of relationship."

"I only wanted to make love to you, not sell you into slavery." His voice was soft yet full of emotion. Lorna had expected him to be irritated by her abrupt termination of their embrace, so she was surprised by the tenderness in his tone. She knew that her own anger was only half real—an outlet for her frustrated desires as much as an expression of her fear of losing her independence.

"The words you used were significant—that you want to make me yours."

"They were just words, a figure of speech." There was a bit of exasperation in his voice now, and she bit her lower lip, wincing as she was sharply reminded of its tender, swollen state.

"You're a poet! Nothing is just words. The words represent your thought, which is that if you made love to me, I'd belong to you. And maybe I would, a little bit. That's precisely why," she continued, talking over his attempt to protest, "I never meant for things to develop to this point. I'm sorry I allowed it to happen."

"But at least you've saved yourself from a fate worse than death."

Lorna shrugged. "I think you know that wasn't what I was saying."

He stood up to tuck his shirt in. "You're just like your damn cactus garden—all dry prickles and sand. You could be lush and green and tender if you'd just relax and let nature take its course."

"And soon I'd be right back where I was four years ago. Unsure of myself, depressed, trying to placate a superior, impatient man who accepted only the finest in everything, including women. No, thanks."

He looked at her strangely, his eyes very dark under his furrowed brow. "None of us wants to go back to old pain or to reopen old wounds. But you can't just deny your own desires. You weren't meant to live alone any more than I was."

Lorna hunched her shoulders as if to ward off his words. It was true. She had allowed herself to believe for a time that with Jason something special was possible. She had been overcome by a sensual need she had long denied, and her body had tricked her into forgetting the promises she had made to herself.

He looked at her silently. "I'll get you some wine," he said at last.

Lorna nodded, suddenly too miserable to speak. Her body now seemed chilled and clumsy, her aching breasts an unwelcome reminder of her recent passionate abandon. She couldn't remember ever having felt so free in lovemaking—until she had forced herself to stop.

"Six puppies and all's well," Jason said quietly, handing her a glass of wine.

"I don't know if I should drink this or not. I'm going to feel lousy enough in the morning as it is."

"It's been a rather difficult evening."

"You want me to be something I'm not."

He put his wine down carefully. "No, I want you to be something you *are*. You're carrying around a man-proof shield to protect yourself against your own femininity. You need to trust your emotions, trust your senses. You won't disintegrate if you let a man get close to you."

She had no immediate answer. Twisting the stem of her wineglass between her fingers, she tried to think rationally about what he was saying.

"There's no such thing as an intimate relationship between equals," she said finally. "One person always has more power than the other, and whoever has the power uses it to dominate the other person."

He looked into his glass, his expression as dour as if the drink had been poisoned. "That's a rather extreme and dogmatic view of relationships. It's not necessarily true. Your ideas seem to be set in concrete, and right now I lack the energy to hack them loose. Let's do the dishes. I'll wash and you dry."

She looked at him in amazement. "Haven't you heard of dishwashers? I guess things are pretty primitive up in Vermont."

"Not really. I just get nostalgic over the wonderful childhood evenings spent in front of the sink, sudsy water and damp flour-sack towels. I thought we could recapture some of that old magic."

"Very poetic, but I have a better idea. Why don't you get some dogfood out of the garage and feed Brandy? I'll bet she's starved by now."

She loaded the dishwasher quickly, and then looked at him uncertainly. "Do you like to play backgammon?"

"No."

She laughed a little. "I don't either, really, but I thought we should do something." She wished he would leave, but she hardly knew how to suggest it.

"Idle hands are the devil's workshop. Difficult to know how to pass the time without making love, isn't it?"

"How about a walk?" she offered, carefully ignoring his gibe. "Did you bring a sweater?"

"In the car. After my weekend at the beach I'm never

going to go anywhere in northern California without warm clothes."

She took a jacket and a flashlight from the hall closet as they left.

"How do you happen to have friends in Carmel?"

"Tom was a senior partner in the law firm until he retired and moved out here. His wife, Miriam, is a painter and she loves to do seascapes. They always spent their vacations in Carmel." They walked along the silent road, circles of light from the flashlight bobbing around their feet. The smell of pine trees permeated the cool, damp air. "It was Tom and Miriam who first showed me what a good marriage could be, I think."

"What about your parents?"

"I suppose they were happy in an old-fashioned sort of way. They didn't expect much, and they didn't get much. My father brought home the money, and my mother took care of the house, children, and friends. I certainly wouldn't model my marriage on them. Would you imitate your parents?"

"No. As long as my dad was alive, Mom seemed only to be his echo. Or maybe his shadow. And he never even seemed to notice her. Then when he died she just withered up and lost interest in life, as if she had no existence without him. Maybe she was an intelligent, vibrant person before she married him, or maybe she was always insubstantial. I'll never know."

"But you don't want to share her fate?"

"Would you?"

"Not from your description. But it sounds as if she loved your father very much. Maybe she was happier than you think."

She was hardly going to argue with him about her own parents, even if he was arrogant enough to think he understood them better than she did.

56

"I can see why you were a successful lawyer."

He shrugged. "I'd like you to meet my friends someday."

"Won't you be going back to Vermont soon?"

"I don't stay there all the time, you know."

"I'm not surprised. I know I would miss having people around."

"The solitude has been very good for me, I think. I had a lot of time to think about what I wanted out of life and how I could go about getting it. And the quiet is great for writing poetry. But I miss the company of women." His teeth flashed briefly in the dark. "Even unwilling ones."

Lorna didn't respond, preoccupied with her own thoughts. She knew she was honestly trying to avoid getting involved with Jason, yet some of her behavior was indeed designed to bring about exactly the involvement she didn't want. Clearly, she had mixed feelings about Jason Coulter. He must be aware of her ambivalence and he probably had his own interpretation of it. She sighed and he took her hand.

"Things will work out. You're halfway there already, I think."

"Where?" she asked sharply, pulling her hand away. "Where you think I should be?"

"That's one way of putting it. I think, given time, you'll realize that not every relationship is a jail cell. Part of you needs just what you say you want to avoid. No one was meant to live alone. And, I might add, for a lady who wants nothing to do with men, you wear rather sexy underwear. It made me think I wasn't the only one who had hopes for this evening. But there won't be any more evenings like this. I'm too old to tolerate being thwarted very often, and too young to resign myself to your celibate wishes."

Their footsteps suddenly sounded loud and ominous in

the quiet, and Lorna felt as if a vacuum were developing in her chest. She had known that Jason was scheduled to return to Vermont at the end of the week. But she had thought they might still have one or two evenings together. She tried to breathe slowly, amazed at the depth of her hurt. They had been so close just a short time ago, it was difficult to believe he could say good-bye this easily.

She forced herself to speak levelly. "Perhaps we could at least have coffee sometime before you go."

"Perhaps." He turned to look at her, but the darkness hid his expression. The strange pain in her chest had eased somewhat, but she still found it difficult to breathe.

"I'm sorry," she said as they reached his rental car, wondering at the same time what she was apologizing for.

"Apologies are not what I want." He touched one knuckle to her cheek, then stroked his finger lightly along her cheekbone while she stood frozen in front of him. With the same finger he traced the edge of her upper lip. It was a tantalizing sensation that left her torn, hardly knowing whether she wanted him to stop or go on. Her lower lip received the same careful outlining, and she was irresistibly reminded of his earlier kisses. What was he trying to do?

Finally his finger moved directly across the center of her lips, somehow satisfying her and yet leaving her longing for much more, for the pressure of his lips, the caresses of his hands on her naked skin. Her lips parted and she stared like a terrified bird into his half-closed eyes as his hand dropped to stroke the soft underside of her chin. He was going to kiss her, she realized with a strange combination of elation and nervousness, and as his lips brushed hers she fell against him, her arms entwined around his neck as if she would never let him go. His lips were insistent, moving softly against hers until he had fully reawakened her earlier passion. He hadn't given up; he was still trying to change her mind.

"I believe you want me as much as I want you," he murmured against her parted lips, and with a low moan she turned her head away and put her arms at her side. His hands were on her shoulder blades, tilting her toward him, and he released her reluctantly.

"So it's still no?" he asked, and she nodded, not trusting her voice.

"It's a terrible pity," he said softly, and pressed his finger once more against the center of her lips. Then he was in the car and gone.

She touched her lips lightly with her fingers as she walked into the house. Mechanically, she let Brandy out for a short time while she checked the puppies and closed up the house for the night, grimacing as she found her lacy bra behind the sofa. Once upstairs, with Brandy safely back in the kitchen, she looked around her bedroom as if she were a stranger. What could he have gathered from the pale gray carpet and the neatly made double bed covered with a bright quilt? The only personal item in view was her picture of Beth and the children. It looked like a motel room, she thought bleakly, and her eyes burned for an instant as if she might cry.

"To hell with him," she said aloud, angrily stripping off her clothes. "Who needs him?" It would be difficult, but she'd have to pull herself together. She didn't need any more misery or self-doubt, nor did she need a man like Jason Coulter. She'd prided herself on her independence, and whatever he thought, she wasn't about to throw herself at his feet and beg him to take her on any terms. Or was she?

"Shape up!" she snarled at her reflection in the mirror, and flung herself into bed.

CHAPTER FOUR

"Are you on the list for the seminar tonight?" Annie asked from the office door.

Lorna looked up from the stack of correspondence on her desk and removed the pencil from her mouth to answer, "What seminar?" she asked, fully aware of which one it was.

Annie leaned back against the wall and assumed a calf-like expression. " 'The Poet in Today's World,' of course. I stood in line for three hours to sign up. Imagine, I'll be in a room with Jason Coulter and only twelve other people. I thought, since you know him, you might have gotten on the list without standing in line."

"No. I won't be there." Lorna scribbled a note to herself and put the pencil back in her mouth as Annie peered at her.

"Why do you always eat your pencils?"

"I'm not eating it," Lorna said with what she thought was admirable restraint, once again removing the pencil. "I'm just keeping it handy. If I put it on my desk, it gets buried, and I waste hours every day patting around trying to find it."

"Well, I'm sure the paint is not good for you."

"Probably not, but as someone who eats potato chips

and lime soda for breakfast, you're hardly in a position to advise me."

Annie returned to her typewriter outside the office, turning at the door to show Lorna the eyes of a wounded doe. At the erratic sound of the typewriter keys, Lorna sighed. She had been a little snappish lately, and it was unfair to Annie. As the end of the academic year approached, there seemed to be thousands of petty chores to do, including a myriad of new forms the administrative dean wanted filled out, and both Annie and Lorna were overworked.

At the sound of the carillon at noon she balanced her pencil carefully on top of the telephone and went to find some lunch. Normally on such a busy day she would bring a sandwich and eat in the office, but since she hadn't taken time to go to the grocery store, the refrigerator at home was empty.

The sky had been clear since early morning and it was quite warm outside. Many of the girls wore sundresses, and Lorna almost envied them, although her own cotton dress had only tiny cap sleeves. She bought some strawberry yogurt and an apple at the campus store, and managed to find a few unoccupied inches of grass by the fountain. Slipping off her sandals, she stretched her legs out to the sun, regretting she had worn panty hose and wishing she were bare-legged.

"Hello."

She squinted up into the light, recognizing the deep voice but still feeling somewhat uncertain at the sight of Jason smiling down at her.

"This is like the beach on the Fourth of July," he muttered, sitting down carefully to avoid contact with his neighbor's elbow. "I haven't seen you lately," he said with an ingenuous smile, and Lorna carefully ate a spoonful of yogurt.

"No," she said finally, "you haven't. I suppose you'll be leaving tomorrow."

He nodded. "But as it turns out, I'll be gone for just a week."

She looked at him more closely, her plastic spoon poised in midair.

"I had dinner with Fred Arnold last night, and he told me that George Terwilliger is ill and won't be able to teach his master poet seminars this summer. Fred asked me to fill in, and I agreed."

Her heart skipped a beat and a rush of happiness swept over her, but she tried to keep her voice steady.

"That's wonderful. I'm sure the students will be delighted."

"I was hoping a certain administrator would be delighted too." He raised his eyebrows, his deep blue eyes watching her so carefully that she began to stir her yogurt as if that were the most important task of her day. As the silence lengthened she looked at the fountain, choosing her words carefully.

"If you mean me, I don't know. I guess I thought I wouldn't be seeing you in any case."

"You'll be seeing me." He picked up her hand where it rested on the grass, slowly caressing the tip of her forefinger with his thumb as he watched her face. She turned away slightly, her fingers twitching nervously, and he gave a soft chuckle, squeezing her hand tightly for an instant and then releasing it.

"There's nothing to be afraid of." He ran one finger slowly down her bare arm, and she shivered, fighting an urge to fold her arms as he took her hand again. He lifted it to brush it with his lips, then let go, standing up easily. "I'd better get ready for my next public appearance. Sunbathing fully clothed leaves much to be desired, I find."

"Since you'll be here for a few months, don't you think you should try to adapt to native habits?"

"Let's just say I'm too old to learn."

She grinned up at him, seeing him only as a dark outline against the brilliant sun.

"I'll call you when I get back," he said as he turned away, and she smiled.

Only time would tell whether he actually intended to call her, she thought as she tossed her yogurt container and apple core into an enormous trash can. But at least he wasn't leaving Crowley, and he hadn't completely forgotten her. Nor she him, she reminded herself uneasily. She returned to her office feeling a little more cheerful, only to find Annie staring morosely at the typewriter.

"Tired fingers?" Lorna asked.

"I'm just not sure I should go to the seminar tonight," Annie said, following Lorna into her office. "Maybe my ignorance will show and I'll be embarrassed."

"Maybe you'll make the most brilliant remark of the evening and everyone will be insanely jealous."

"Yeah." Annie seemed lost in thought, apparently enjoying the fantasy as she walked slowly back to her desk. After a minute the sound of typing came once again to Lorna's ears.

The next morning Annie was already hard at work when Lorna arrived. "How did it go?" she asked as she passed the desk, and Annie stopped typing to shrug.

"I never opened my mouth. The competition was too stiff for me, I guess. There was enough eyeshadow in the room to paint a building, and you could smell the perfume all the way down the hall." Lorna laughed as Annie went on. "All I did was wear my best jeans, and I felt like a kindergartener in a group of debutantes."

"I doubt that Jason Coulter was impressed by the debutantes."

"Maybe not." Annie sighed. "At least I got his autograph. And I got to see him up close. Do you suppose he gets tired of all the female fans panting after him?"

"I wouldn't know." Lorna retired to her office, sighing as she confronted the stacks of papers on her desk.

"Got a minute?" Fran came in and closed the office door, a gesture unusual enough to make Lorna sit up a little straighter.

"Anything wrong?"

Fran sat down in a straight-backed chair pulled up beside the desk. "I'm not sure. Have you had any run-ins with Dean Allen, the new administrative dean?"

Lorna shook her head. "I've never even met the man, and I've carefully refrained from telling him what he can do with all these forms and checklists." She gestured at the papers on her desk.

"Have you said anything about him to anyone?"

"No, I've been too busy even to complain."

Fran sighed. "Well, I'm not sure about this, it's just a rumor, but the word is that he's making noises about you being unqualified for this job."

Lorna suppressed a spurt of anger by taking a deep breath. "As long as he confines himself to making noises, I suppose I'd better ignore him."

"I guess. I didn't want to worry you, but I thought you should keep it in mind."

Lorna nodded soberly. "I'll be on my best behavior."

"Everyone knows you do a wonderful job," Fran said suddenly. "I'm sorry I even mentioned it." She opened the office door again. "I'm sure it's nothing to worry about."

She left abruptly and Lorna turned to look out her window at the familiar view. This was the first time her qualifications had been questioned, and it unsettled her.

Her job had come to her easily—she hadn't had to fight for it, but she would now, if it became necessary.

It had turned out to be a nice clear day for Jason's flight home, she thought suddenly. A pair of laughing students passed just under her window, their arms around each other's waists, and she watched them a little wistfully, then turned again to her desk and began searching for her pencil. Qualified or not, she'd better get rid of some of her paperwork before it buried the telephone.

Two hours later she shoved a random bunch of papers into her briefcase and took them home for the weekend. After all, she told herself sternly, she had nothing to do all weekend except buy groceries, do the laundry, clean house, and attend one concert and one lecture. There would be plenty of time to catch up on her work. If Dean Allen hoped to intimidate her by his coils of red tape, she would show him what she was made of.

On Monday she returned to the office, half expecting that several new mounds of papers would have appeared on her desk over the weekend. Things were not quite as bad as she had feared, however, and by taking work home with her for several nights she was able to bring things back to normal. By Friday, when the Woebegone Werewolves were due to arrive, her desk was almost cleared.

Late that morning a group of red-eyed, unshaven young men appeared in her office and announced that they were ready to set up their equipment in the amphitheater. With some trepidation Lorna sent Annie to guide them and called the Starlight Motel to see if the Werewolves themselves had checked in.

"Everything's nailed to the floor or chained to the wall," the motel manager informed her. "We're ready, but they haven't shown up yet. Shall I have them call you when they do?"

"No, just give them my number if they want me." She hung up briskly and began working on emptying her In basket.

At lunchtime, when Annie still had not returned, Lorna decided to stroll over to the amphitheater to make sure things were going smoothly. Finding Annie cheerfully strewing wires with one of the better-looking young men, she shrugged and returned to the administration building. Everything seemed to be well under control. The telephone in her office greeted her with a sharp ring, and she picked it up with a presentiment of disaster. While she listened, doodling tight circles on a piece of paper, Jason Coulter appeared in the doorway and leaned smiling against the doorjamb.

She managed a brief smile after she hung up, then bent to get her purse out of the bottom desk drawer. "Welcome back."

He frowned. "Are you running out on me? I came to invite you to lunch."

"I have to take care of the Werewolves before the manager calls the police."

Jason's eyebrows rose several inches. "Do you have much trouble with werewolves and vampires on the campus?"

"It's a group," Lorna explained. "Sort of a musical group, to be charitable. They're giving a concert tonight —if I can keep them out of jail long enough."

"Can I come along?"

Lorna eyed him speculatively. "Why not? You might even be big enough to intimidate them."

She drove quickly to the motel, shifting jerkily and muttering all the way. When she'd made arrangements for the concert, she had been turned down by several

convenient motels. The manager of the Starlight, however, had been quite eager to accommodate the Werewolves as long as they agreed to pay for any damage. A
burly man with tattoos on each arm, he had seemed well
able to take care of himself, and Lorna had been very
pleased, particularly since she had scheduled the concert
on such short notice. Now that the Werewolves had actually arrived, it was a fine time for him to be having second thoughts.

The deafening waves of rock music became audible
about a block away from the motel, and Lorna rolled up
her window with a grimace. She could almost see the air
vibrating, and she looked at Jason apologetically. "I
don't suppose you came equipped with earplugs. Shall I
drop you off here to save you from deafness?"

He shrugged. "No, if you can stand it, I suppose I
can."

Further speech became impossible as she pulled into
the motel parking lot, and they hurried from the car into
the inadequate protection of the small, shabby office. The
noise of the music was exacerbated by the rhythmic rat-
tling of plate glass windows, and Lorna pressed her
hands against her ears. She looked helplessly at the manager, who was seated at a scarred wooden desk behind
the counter. Recognizing her, he stood up slowly and
came to lean over the counter.

"They've chained the door and taken the phone off the
hook," he bellowed into her left ear. "I'll give you five
minutes to think of something, then I'm calling the police. Two people have already checked out."

"Do you have a bolt cutter?" Lorna screamed, and
scowled when he shook his head.

With her hands firmly covering her ears, she went out
to reconnoiter, closely followed by the two men. The mu-

sic was pouring through a small, half-open window in the beige stucco wall. She pointed at it questioningly.

"Bathroom," the manager confirmed, looking at her doubtfully. "Will you fit?"

Lorna shrugged as the manager produced an aluminum ladder. She climbed up carefully, glad she was wearing slacks, and peeked cautiously through the window, praying that the bathroom would be empty. The Werewolves might not be dressed for visitors, she realized suddenly. But she'd have to take her chances. Unless the manager . . . She looked down at his protruding stomach and squared her shoulders. This was her job, and she was stuck with it.

She twisted the screen out and reached inside to crank the window completely open, then sat down gingerly on the windowsill and lowered herself carefully into the chipped green bathtub, which turned out to be full of melting ice cubes and a large variety of canned beer. Her sandals squishing and the bottoms of her pants clinging damply to her ankles, she went tentatively into the orange and gold bedroom. It was empty, and she walked through the connecting door to the next room, which boasted a color scheme of olive green and dark blue. There sat the five Werewolves in a tight circle around a giant cassette player, their fingers snapping and heads jerking rhythmically. Feeling a little like a heroine in a spy movie, Lorna ignored their astonished looks, threw herself on the player, and turned it off.

The silence was stunning. She removed the batteries from the back of the player and put them into her purse. Then she examined her audience with interest. Two had crewcuts, one's head was completely shaved, and two had very long uncombed hair. All were dressed identically in faded jeans and torn muscle shirts, and all had what appeared to be a two-day growth of beard, which was in stark contrast to their liberal applications of electric blue eyeshadow.

"Hey, lady," the bald Werewolf said plaintively. "We were listening to that."

"So was everyone else within a mile of here," Lorna replied, unchaining the door to admit Jason and the manager. "I'm Lorna Phillips, the one who booked the concert."

"I'm Beo," a young man with a crewcut announced.

Lorna extended her hand, but allowed it to fall to her side as Beo scratched his head.

"We need to get in the mood for tonight," Beo told her. "That's why we were playing the music."

As the manager moved forward, one of the group stood protectively in front of the cassette player. "If you don't give us back our batteries, we won't go on tonight."

"Yeah," the others agreed, seeming to feel they had found the perfect threat.

Lorna was tempted by a momentary dream of canceling the concert and leaving the Werewolves to their own devices, but she pulled herself together. "I'll get you four more cassette players and five sets of earphones," she offered.

The five Werewolves went into a huddle as she glanced at Jason. He was sitting contentedly in a straight-backed chair in front of a desk, apparently enjoying the performance. Now that she had a moment to think, Lorna tried to decide what else needed to be done. At least the Werewolves had confined themselves to drinking beer, she realized, and nothing was broken yet. There was much to be grateful for. The muttered conference seemed to be drawing to a conclusion, and she waited expectantly. Beo approached her, seeming to search for the words he needed to express himself.

He breathed deeply several times, stared down at his

bare toes, then looked up into her eyes. "Okay," he said, and Lorna gave him a brilliant smile.

"I'll get things under way right now," she promised, hoping that Annie had returned to the office by now. With the Werewolves in a claustrophobic circle around her, she dialed her number and grinned as Annie answered. Having instructed her to beg or borrow the necessary equipment and rush it to the motel, Lorna looked up at the five expectant faces. Apparently she would have to entertain them until Annie arrived.

"Have you had lunch?"

They shook their heads.

"Well, then," she said, carefully avoiding Jason's gaze. "Jason and I were just about to go to lunch. Why don't you come with us? And you too." She gestured grandly to include the motel manager, who shook his head.

"I think there's a place right down the road here. If you want to get your jackets. And shoes," she added. "We can probably get some hamburgers or something." She smiled brightly at Jason, who was now scowling fiercely.

"I have to keep them busy," she whispered as the Werewolves wandered in and out, searching for their clothes with apparent lack of success.

"Couldn't you have had something delivered? I'm not sure the general public is ready to face them at lunch."

Lorna shrugged, having decided to harden her heart against all pleas. "The public will just have to suffer, and be grateful they didn't see them at breakfast. And I'm hardly a vision of loveliness myself." She pointed to her soggy ankles. "If you'd rather, you can wait here for Annie. I'm sure she'd be delighted to drive you back to the campus."

"And leave you alone with them?" Jason shook his head.

"I'm sure they're very nice young men, underneath all that . . ." Words failed her.

"I'd feel better if they looked nicer right on the surface," Jason replied. "It's occurred to me, though, that in order for them to look as if they haven't shaved for two days, they have to be clean-shaven at some point. Quite an intriguing thought. Do you suppose they hide in their houses until they have enough beard growth to look horrible?"

"They probably have special punk razors to give the effect," Lorna whispered as the Werewolves returned, resplendent in satin jackets and torn athletic shoes.

"Don't you all look nice," Lorna said. Then feeling a little like a den mother, she led her troop down the street to the closest fast-food restaurant. She watched maternally as the Werewolves ate the equivalent of three lunches and four bottles of ketchup apiece. Jason's appetite, not surprisingly, was less hearty. Lorna herself ended up giving away most of her lunch to Beo, who seemed to find everything that came from her tray particularly appealing.

"You'd better be careful," Jason said as they led the way back to the motel. "Beo's already got a crush on you."

"Well, I think he's cute," Lorna said, almost resenting Jason's amused smile.

"You like the silent type?"

She shrugged. "It's true that he doesn't talk much, but on the other hand he finds other ways of making his presence known. Anyway, they're barely out of their teens. Frankly, I expected much worse."

The motel parking lot came into view, and Lorna was relieved to see Annie's old Volkswagen. The cassette players must have arrived. "I wonder if I should stay here until the concert," Lorna murmured, heading toward the Werewolves' room.

Jason rolled his eyes. "Surely that would be beyond the call of duty."

"Nothing is beyond the call of duty," she informed him sternly. They watched the Werewolves drape themselves happily around the room, pulling their earphones over their heads. With an apologetic smile Lorna removed the batteries from her purse and handed them over to the boy who had inherited the original cassette player. "This looks quite peaceful, don't you think?"

"Let's leave while we can," Jason agreed, and Lorna beckoned to Annie.

"Would you like me to stay with them?" Annie asked.

Lorna beamed. "That would be ideal. Just deliver them at seven o'clock sharp."

"They're cute, in a weird sort of way," Annie whispered, and Jason shook his head.

Once she and Jason were back in the car, Lorna hesitated before pulling out of the parking lot. "Would you like another lunch?" she asked.

"No, I guess I just wasn't hungry after all."

She glanced at him quickly. "You wanted to come."

"Yes, and it was quite an education. I can see you're more accustomed than I to the idiosyncrasies of the younger generation."

"One has to be to work on a college campus," she replied, pulling into her parking space. "Maybe this isn't where you wanted to go—can I take you somewhere?"

"No, I think I'll walk back to the cottage and quietly contemplate the rise and fall of civilizations."

"Aren't you taking the Werewolves a little too seriously?"

"Maybe. I can't decide whether to be horrified or amused."

"Probably they're very bright, well-mannered young men, and all this is just an act they have to put on to be stars. Or at least that's what I tell myself."

He laughed. "I can see that you'd have to tell yourself something. And I enjoyed watching you in action—sort of a combination of Wonder Woman and Mary Poppins."

"Fortunately, I rarely have to crawl through windows, or I wouldn't last long at my job." Her smile faded as she suddenly remembered what Fran had said about the administrative dean. Jason leaned toward her.

"What's the matter?"

"Nothing." She flapped her hands sideways. "I just thought of something I need to get straightened out, that's all."

She looked at him fully for the first time that day. With some surprise she realized that she had been so preoccupied with the Werewolves that she had accepted his presence without a thought. Now that she had time to think, she became self-conscious, remembering their earlier intimacies. She felt the tingle of anxiety in her stomach and took a deep breath.

"Are you back for the summer?"

"More or less." He leaned against the door of the car, seeming even more relaxed by contrast to her own sudden agitation. "I may go back to Vermont once or twice, just to keep an eye on things."

"Will you be happy in the guest cottage, or would you like to look for another place?"

He shrugged. "The cottage will be fine. It's convenient and inoffensive."

"It's not exactly charming and full of character," she agreed, then fell silent as he watched her.

"I've been thinking about where we go from here," he said finally, and she glanced away, studying the gauges

73

behind the steering wheel. "Shall I tell you my thoughts?"

He was smiling, and she took another breath, wishing she could be as comfortable as he seemed to be. "Of course," she said, struggling to sound casual. "But please keep in mind that I might have a few ideas of my own."

"With any luck, we may even agree. My idea is to give you some breathing space, let you get used to the idea of having me around. Who knows, you may even decide you like it."

Perversely, she felt slightly let down. "I can't make any promises." She looked over his shoulder at the steps of the administration building, watching staff and students come and go. His fingers touched her lightly just above her elbow, and she looked at him.

He turned to lean toward her, still touching her arm but not holding it and she found herself swaying closer, her lips slightly parted. For a long breath their mouths didn't touch, until she shifted in her seat to allow his lips to brush hers lightly back and forth.

He moved away and she straightened quickly, her hand on the door handle, her face a little warm.

"Give me a call if you like, or I may drop in at your office some day." He looked at her unsmilingly and she nodded, still feeling the soft imprint of his kiss. Then, as she opened her door, he was out of the car and gone, walking rapidly through the crowd of students.

Lorna sighed and locked her car, hardly aware of what she was doing. She went slowly up the stairs to her office, one hand trailing along the wooden bannister, and she sat down heavily in her chair, spinning around to look blindly out the window. She remembered the sensation of Jason's lips on hers, the heat of his mouth. She closed her eyes.

"How are the Werewolves?" Fran's voice made her swing around guiltily.

"You know, for a few minutes I'd almost forgotten them. Annie's keeping an eye on things, in the absence of a nursemaid. Next year I hope the sophomore class has more conservative tastes."

Fran nodded, running her fingers through her dark curly hair. "Alice said that Dean Allen is preparing a letter to you."

"Well, good for him. What is it about?" Lorna began to straighten the edges of the papers on her desk.

"That's not clear yet, but it won't be good news."

Lorna sighed. "Well, if he's going to fire me, he could have done it yesterday and saved me a trip to the Starlight Motel. Not to mention ruptured eardrums and wet ankles."

"I'm glad you can be cheerful about it, but I'm worried."

Lorna shrugged. "So am I. But what can I do? I just have to sit back and wait for the bad news. Then I'll know what I'm fighting."

"I'm going to think of something better than that," Fran said. "And I'll let you know."

Settling down to work, Lorna began to plow her way doggedly through the stack of correspondence in her basket. She jotted down several replies for Annie and stacked them neatly in the bottom basket. When the sounds of people leaving for home began to penetrate her office, she looked at her watch. She'd better check up on things at the amphitheater. Too often there were last-minute hitches—a forgotten extension cord, a broken plug, a snapped guitar string. Scowling at the wrinkled hems of her slacks, she stood up and gave her chair a hard twirl. She'd been in the office long enough.

She drove slowly to the amphitheater through the evening traffic. Once inside the gate, she noted that most of the sound crew seemed to be lying on the grass drinking beer. A sign that all was well, she thought. The head of the crew confirmed that everything was ready, and Lorna headed home.

It was difficult to know what to wear to the concert besides earplugs and a stadium blanket, she thought. It could be miserably cold sitting on the grass once the sun had set, and even the huge bowl of the amphitheater would not preclude the music swelling out at top volume. With a twist of her lips she selected a pair of pale pink corduroy slacks and a heavy cableknit sweater. She'd probably stand out like a sore thumb among all the blue denim, but if she wrapped the blanket around her, no one would notice.

After a quick omelette and a spinach salad, she drove back to the campus, leaving her car at her office. From there she walked to the amphitheater to avoid some of the concert traffic. As she showed her pass at the gate, a familiar voice murmured, "I'd recognize you anywhere, even when you're all bundled up."

"It's your hair," Jason explained as she turned around. "In this light it's nearly white."

"And there aren't many white-haired old ladies out tonight," Lorna noted, smiling as she looked at the crowd around her.

"Do you sit on that blanket, or do you wear it?" he asked.

"Both." Lorna led the way to a spot as far from the bandstand as possible and began arranging the plaid blanket. "Did you actually pay money to come here, after this morning?"

"I was curious," Jason said. "I wanted to see if they had shaved. I assume I'm allowed to leave in the middle if I choose."

76

"They'll probably lock us in here. Did you want to share my blanket?" she offered belatedly as he sat down next to her.

"Let's just see if we both fit." He gathered the corners of the blanket and brought them across their shoulders and around their knees. "I'm sure this is possible."

Lorna looked skeptically at her two corners but moved obediently next to him while he arranged and rearranged the folds of the blanket.

"There," he announced finally. "All you have to do is lean back against me a little more and all the ends will meet."

Lorna laughed. "Now, if you just had a giant safety pin, we'd be quite cozy."

"I'll hold the edges together until intermission," he said, "and then it will be your turn." Smiling, she allowed her head to tuck under his chin, feeling his breath ruffle her hair. His right arm curved warmly around her waist under the blanket, tightening convulsively as the music began.

The concert was louder and less comprehensible than she had expected, although the wild applause indicated that all was well as far as the audience was concerned. More and more Lorna found herself oblivious to the noise and the crowd, warm with Jason in their small cocoon. The rise and fall of his chest, his heartbeat against her back, were the only rhythms she was aware of. At some point during the evening she had laid her right arm over his, so that her hand rested on his wrist. Her own breathing seemed to adjust easily to his, and she sighed as his hand moved idly up and down her waist through the bulk of her sweater. The sky was clear and full of stars and she looked upward, deaf to the pounding music.

His fingers brushed the bare skin under her ribs and she tightened her grip on his wrist for an instant, relaxing as he continued the same undemanding caress. Her body seemed to throb to the beat of his heart. As he stroked her waist she felt suspended in time, wondering if his hand would move upward to caress her breasts, or lower to reach beneath the waistband of her slacks. The skin below her ribs became increasingly sensitive, anticipating the silken brush of his fingertips up and down, higher and lower. Her right hand moved on the back of his wrist, barely playing with the fine hairs there. Her breasts grew full, aching to share in the sensation of his touch, which seemed to retreat maddeningly each time his knuckles brushed the bottom of the soft swell.

She hadn't worn a bra, since she'd known she would be thoroughly bundled up in her sweater and blanket. If his hand moved just a few inches, it would cover her breast, satisfying the growing need she felt for more intimate contact. She moved her left hand under the blanket and found his thigh, firm beneath the blue denim. Cautiously she rested her palm on his knee, her thumb moving tentatively against the hollow at the side of his kneecap. His caress moved upward then, his fingers playing delicately along the lower curve of first one breast, then the other. Restlessly she shifted against him, sliding a little lower, her hand rubbing urgently up and down his thigh. It was growing very warm beneath the stadium blanket, and her heart was hammering against his hand. She tilted her head back into the hollow of his neck, arching her back, and sighed with satisfaction as finally, with tantalizing slowness, his fingers circled upward.

Still he avoided her nipples and she shifted again, wanting his touch so much that she no longer felt a need for caution. With her right hand she gripped his wrist firmly, impelling it upward as her body slid to meet his fingers, to end the teasing restraint he was exercising. He bent his head then, his lips moving tenderly beneath her ear and down her neck, leaving an electric trail that caused her hand to tighten over his.

And then the sound of applause penetrated their private world. She turned to him, her cheeks hot, and he brought his mouth back up to her lips, his hands taking leave of her swollen breasts with seeming reluctance. She hated for the moment to end. With a sudden twist she pressed herself tightly against him, forcing their mouths together in a long, bruising kiss. He was still for a moment, his heart beating heavily against her, and then he gripped her shoulders and pushed her away a few inches, smiling at her upturned face. "Maybe I should attend your rock concerts more often."

Lorna smoothed down her hair self-consciously. "Did you enjoy it?"

He laughed. "I'm afraid I didn't pay much attention to the music. What about you?"

"I didn't either," she admitted, watching the surrounding students shake out and fold their blankets. "I guess it's time to go. Somehow I missed intermission."

Jason frowned. "Maybe they played straight through. It's miraculous that we could be bombarded by all that noise and not take any of it in. A testament to our mutual preoccupation."

Temporary insanity would be a better description, she thought as she pushed away the edges of the blanket and stood up. Somehow, in her happiness that Jason was there beside her, she had forgotten all the promises she had made to herself. Everything had happened so naturally, so delightfully, that for a time she had forgotten her fears about getting involved with him.

She watched silently, biting her lower lip, as Jason folded the large blanket into a neat square. Her mind was working again now that his arms were no longer around her, and she had completely lost the euphoric, abandoned

79

feeling she had enjoyed when they were wrapped together in the blanket. She was astonished that she had let things progress so far. It must seem to Jason as if she habitually made promises of intimacy that she had no intention of keeping. How could he ever understand her behavior when she herself was confused by it? One minute she was overwhelmed by her attraction to him and everything was magically right. The next minute she was frightened of the power he had over her, unwilling to let him come closer.

They walked out slowly at the rear of the chattering crowd, each lost in thought until Lorna stopped at her car. She unlocked her door, then stood awkwardly. "Would you like a ride to the cottage?"

His thumbs caressed her cheekbones, then his fingers swooped into her hair, tilting her face upward. "I think you know what I'd like."

She shook her head numbly, feeling his hands drop to her shoulders. "I can't do that right now. I'm just . . ." Her voice rose dangerously and she stopped. She didn't know the right words to explain her feelings.

"Was it your marriage that was so bad, or your divorce?"

"I don't know," she whispered. "Maybe there's just something wrong with me."

He pulled her against him, his arms firmly around her back. Her head rested against his shoulder, and she sighed as with one hand he stroked the muscles around her spine.

"I'm trying to understand," he said after several minutes, "but I don't know you very well yet. Do you need more time?"

"I just feel very shaky about a lot of things right now," she said. "My job, my whole life. And I'm afraid to take

80

any chances. I can't promise that it will change with time."

"I suppose that's the risk I'll have to take." He smoothed her hair tenderly as they moved apart. "If you won't come to the cottage tonight . . ." He paused, and she shook her head, wishing she had the courage to say yes.

"Then I'll walk back," he said. "Good night."

"Good night." Lorna slid behind the steering wheel and closed the door, then rolled down her window as he turned to walk away. "I'm glad you're back," she called softly, and he smiled.

"Good. So am I."

Slowly she closed the window, then rested her head against the seat for a few seconds before starting the engine. She could still drive to his cottage. . . . She shook her head and backed out of her parking place. Twenty minutes later she was surprised to find that she was entering her garage. She had been in a daze the whole drive home.

"This won't do at all," she told herself sternly as she unlocked the door to her house. "Daydreaming will not be tolerated."

She paused in the dark at the foot of the staircase, trying to visualize Jason's face, then grimaced and ran quickly up the stairs.

CHAPTER FIVE

The brown interoffice envelope shook slightly in Lorna's fingers as she spoke into the phone. "Fran, can you come and hold my hand?"

"I'm on my way," Fran replied briskly.

Lorna sank into her chair, the skin on her face tight and painful as she waited. When Fran appeared in the doorway, Lorna's attempted smile turned out to be a grimace and she bit her lip.

Fran closed the door gently behind her. "Is that the letter from Dean Allen? What does it say?"

"I haven't opened it yet," Lorna said. "but I think this is it."

Fran ruffled her dark curls with both hands. "Do you want me to read it first and break the news to you gently?"

"No, just keep me company." Lorna tore the sealed envelope, which had been marked Personal and Confidential, open at one end, pulled out the letter, and glanced quickly through its two paragraphs, her heart thudding as she reached the conclusion.

Her voice cracked as she said to Fran, "He recommends that I take an unpaid leave of absence and go back to school." She tossed the paper across the desk to Fran, who read it for herself.

" 'Your lack of a college degree indicates that you have neither the perseverance nor the cultural awareness the job requires,' " Fran read with a rising inflection, sinking down into a black fabric chair. "What does he know about it?"

"Well, he knows I didn't finish school, and he's drawing conclusions from that." Lorna bit her thumbnail. "In a way he's right. I was a fool to drop out like that just because I got married. It was what Ward wanted, so as usual I just went along. It was a mistake, and now I'm paying for it." Her chest was tight, but at least her heart had stopped racing.

"You mean you're going to knuckle under to this?" Fran's brown eyes were wide as she waved the letter.

Lorna shrugged, feeling tears sting her eyes. "I love this job, and I want to keep it. And I certainly can't afford a year without pay. Anyway, I've taken dozens of courses, here and at the university, since I started the job. That ought to demonstrate some cultural awareness." She was beginning to grow angry now, and she sat up a little straighter. "I think I'll make up a list of all the courses I've taken, just for his information."

Fran nodded, putting the letter carefully back on the desk. "What about persistence and perseverance?"

Lorna laughed, surprising herself. "I could get testimonials, I suppose. But maybe one of my old phone logs would do. I know that some guests have required an incredible number of calls before I could get them lined up, and that's all marked down. Since forms are so dear to the dean, maybe I'll just copy all my logs for the past three years and let him read them to his heart's content."

"Pompous old ass," Fran muttered suddenly, and

when Lorna grinned, she added, "I don't see how you can smile when this joker is attacking you."

"Because I'm beginning to think I can win." Lorna found a clean sheet of paper and began making a list. "What else do I need to prove?"

Fran studied the letter. "Well, he's willing to grant that you may be intelligent and industrious. Oh, yes, here's a hint that you may be a bad example—encouraging students to think they can still get good jobs even if they don't finish college."

"Well, he put his foot in it there. Crowley has one of the lowest dropout rates in the country, so my influence can't be damaging too many academic careers."

Fran stood up. "It looks as if you've got everything under control."

Lorna looked up from her list, then impulsively walked around the desk to hug her friend briefly. "Thank you for coming. I really didn't want to face it by myself."

Fran smiled. "Any time. I'm just glad to see you're going to give him a run for his money. And I'll bet he'll back down in the end."

"Well, if not, at least I can make him wish he'd never started this." She went back to her desk, rapidly noting any evidence she could think of that might influence the dean's opinion. But gathering everything together would take time, and she couldn't afford to slack off at work. She'd have to prepare her rebuttal in the evening. That way she'd be able to do herself justice.

Resolutely she tucked the letter in her briefcase and went back to her work. It took several hours, however, to put the administrative dean firmly in the back of her mind and really concentrate on checking over the letters Annie had typed. It was a relief when the workday was finally over and she could start composing her defense. As the building slowly emptied, Lorna began searching through her filing cabinets for the evidence she planned to present, tossing bundles of papers into her briefcase until it was so full it refused to close.

The next morning she returned hollow-eyed but with a firm letter carefully written, complete with attached telephone logs, lists of courses, and statistics on dropouts. Hesitantly, she approached Annie, who was already typing.

"I'd like to ask you to do something for me that might not be strictly your job."

Annie looked up with a raised eyebrow, and Lorna smiled. "It's nothing exciting, just a typing job. I'd like it to look nice, not all full of corrections."

"Sure." Annie took the letter and glanced at the opening paragraph.

"And let's send a copy to President Arnold too," Lorna decided. "No point in being overly scrupulous."

"Of course not." Annie quickly rolled a fresh sheet of paper into her typewriter. "If there's anything else I can do, please let me know."

Lorna retired to her office, where she sat tapping her pencil against the desk. Now that she had written the letter, she was impatient for the dean and the president to read it and respond. Waiting would be difficult when so much was at stake.

She looked up, startled, as Jason came in, closing the door carefully behind him. "I leave you alone for a few days, and look what happens. Annie told me about the dean," he said as he sat down, and Lorna slammed her pencil down.

"She was wrong to tell you. It's strictly a personal matter."

"Not terribly personal, I think. You hinted at it the other evening. The dean's taken it into his head to make you miserable, and he's succeeding. You're not at fault.

85

Why should you slink around and try to keep it quiet?" He sat down in the chair across from her, his eyes never leaving her face.

Lorna shrugged. "No particular reason, I guess."

"Right. I understand you're writing a letter, but I'd like to call Fred Arnold right now and get the whole mess straightened out. Since Fred's an old friend of mine, I can easily put in a good word for you."

Lorna studied her fingernails for several seconds. "It's nice of you to offer," she said slowly, "but I don't want to owe my job to your friendship with the president. It's important to me that I got this position on my own, because I'm good at it. I want to keep it for the same reason."

"No one's questioning your competence. I just think I can make things happen faster and more smoothly if you'll let me help."

"Just let me handle it myself, please. I have to know I can."

Jason looked at her. "If you're sure that's what you want."

She nodded. "I don't mean to seem ungrateful. But I'm sure."

"Well, I came to see if I could take you to dinner, but perhaps this isn't the ideal time for you."

She paused. It was tempting to think she could curl up against Jason's chest tonight and listen to him tell her that everything would be all right. He would be sympathetic to her fears, she knew. But this time she needed to ride the storm out without a man to lean on, if only to prove to herself that she had changed.

"I don't think I'd be good company right now. But when this is all taken care of, we can go to a really nice restaurant and celebrate, okay?" As he agreed she added,

"Promise you won't get involved in this behind my back."

He held his hand up solemnly. "I said I wouldn't, and I won't. There wouldn't be anything wrong in my helping though. That's how the game is played."

"It's not what you know, it's who you know," Lorna intoned. "I'll keep your offer in mind as a last resort."

He came around her desk and gripped her shoulders firmly for a moment, looking directly into her eyes. His fingers trailed lightly down her arms, awakening her skin as they moved to her wrists. As she closed her eyes he took both her hands and held them. This man was able to reach through her anxieties and make her lose herself in the power of his touch.

"Are you sure I can't help you in any way?" he asked softly. When she opened her eyes he was smiling as if he knew how strongly she was drawn to him. She licked her lips, willing herself to ask him to stay with her, take her to dinner, make love to her until she forgot everything but him. But no words escaped her constricted throat, and the moment passed abruptly when he let go of her hands.

"You're the only one who can knock down the barriers between us," he told her.

She nodded. "I know. Maybe when I know about my job . . ."

"Call me as soon as you hear anything," he said, and she nodded.

He kissed her lightly on the cheek and was gone as she stood staring at the doorway. Slowly she walked out to Annie's desk, one hand ruffling her hair.

"Annie," she began, and the brunette hunched her shoulders protectively.

"I know. But I told him anyway, I was so mad. And I knew he'd want to help."

Lorna shrugged. "Don't do it again."

She felt a little churlish, but life would be difficult if Annie felt free to confide all Lorna's troubles to Jason—or anyone else, for that matter. Back in her office, she watched the students sitting around the fountain, reading, talking, wiggling their fingers in the water. It was another clear, warm day, and the campus seemed shiny and cheerful. If the dean had his way, she would have to find another job. And she would miss the campus and the students, she knew, and even all the eccentric guests. She rested her forehead against the cool window for a moment, fighting a wave of pessimism. There was Jason, she realized suddenly, crossing the courtyard surrounded by a determined band of female students who were thrusting books at him for autographs. He apparently was having his problems, too, Lorna thought as she watched him smile apologetically at the girls and speed off toward his cottage. She sat back down at her desk and picked up the telephone.

The following day Fran stopped by, looking very cool in a turquoise shirtwaist. "Heard anything yet?"

Lorna shook her head. "I guess there hasn't been time, although if he had answered immediately, I might have received the reply this afternoon."

"He'll take his time about it, I'm sure." Fran sighed. "I don't know how you can be so patient."

"What choice do I have?" Lorna began to straighten up her desk. She had thought of little but her letter to the new dean since she had put it in the campus mail, and the idea that she might have to wait indefinitely for a reply was disheartening. Each time she heard the slap of the twice-daily mail delivery on Annie's desk, her stomach tightened and her heart seemed to stop for a second. So far she had resisted the temptation to rush out and paw through the letters herself, and Annie was thoughtful enough to immediately bring in everything addressed personally to Lorna.

She looked down at her skirt, gaily flowered with pink and yellow tulips. Her mood matched neither the weather nor her clothing, although she had deliberately selected the most cheerful thing she owned, pairing the skirt with a bright pink blouse. Usually she could lift her spirits with such small things, but the problem she was facing was not one she could ignore so easily.

Having cleared her desk, she left the building and walked briskly down the sidewalk to the small lot where she had left her car. On the way home, she suddenly thought of Jason, wishing she hadn't postponed their next meeting until she had heard from the dean. If it turned out that she lost her job, she wouldn't call Jason and tell him, she knew. And that would probably mean she would never see him again. It seemed as if she did nothing but wait, unable to focus her attention on anything but an unknown day when her entire future would be decided.

That evening she called her sister, Beth, to tell her about the dean's letter, and was buoyed only temporarily by Beth's certainty that everything would work out in her favor. As the evening wore on, Lorna became increasingly convinced that her situation was hopeless. Unable to concentrate on a magazine she had picked up, she ended up spending three hours staring mindlessly at the television. Then she closed the windows and went to bed, pulling the quilt up under her chin.

The next four days were annoyingly similar, and Lorna began to fantasize calling the dean's secretary to see if he had received her letter. Or perhaps sending Annie out to pick up some gossip. Fran, usually a reliable source of information, hadn't heard even a whisper of news.

The following week Lorna was reading her mail when

Bradley Daniels, a professor in the drama department, came into her office and sat down. "I hear you'll be leaving us soon, and I wanted to tell you how sorry I am."

Lorna looked at him sharply. "I have no plans to leave," she said, struggling to sound nonchalant.

"Oh." Bradley seemed flustered. "I was at a party the other night, and I heard something . . ."

Lorna frowned. Obviously word was getting around that the dean intended to get rid of her. "Can you tell me any more about what you heard?" she asked.

He lifted his hands. "It was nothing, really. Obviously I misunderstood. Anyway, I'm glad you'll be staying."

"Thank you," she said dully as he left. Things were beginning to look rather bleak.

With little of her usual enthusiasm she drove to the airport to meet Professor James Austin, who was to lecture on Trollope that evening. She arrived in plenty of time, and was stunned when all the passengers on the flight walked right by her without even an inquiring glance. As a last hope, she had him paged, and soon a bass voice informed her that he was Professor Austin and that he was in the bar.

"Don't move," Lorna said firmly. "I'll be right there."

Her steps slowed as she neared the bar. The only man there, a burly redhead in horn-rimmed glasses, was leaning heavily on the counter. And she was sure he had not been on the flight she had met.

"Professor Austin?" she asked timidly, and he nodded wisely. "You weren't on the plane I met. Did I get the flights confused?"

"I took an earlier one. I was at a party until this morning, and somehow it didn't seem worth going all the way home. So"—he tossed down the last of what Lorna hoped was only tomato juice—"I just jumped on a plane and here I am." He turned to face her, spreading his arms, and seemed to sway slightly.

"Here you are," Lorna confirmed, her heart sinking. "No luggage?"

"No luggage." He grinned at her in what he probably thought was an engaging way. "No lecture notes."

She stifled a curse. "Let's get you to the campus," she said briskly, taking his elbow.

"Fine." He gave a prolonged yawn while Lorna averted her gaze from the pink interior of his mouth. "Drop me off at the library and I'll put some notes together."

"Good idea." She sounded a lot more confident than she felt, she reflected as she unlocked her car. "Would you like to stop for some coffee?"

"Coffee?" he boomed. "Coffee would keep me awake!" His rumbling laugh filled the car, and Lorna managed a stiff smile. A very funny man. How had she come to invite him here? The lecture promised to be a disaster she would remember for a long time. This was the last thing she needed right at a time when her job was on the line.

She looked despairingly at her passenger as he tilted his seat back and closed his eyes. Once his lecture was over, she'd go through her files and put rude remarks next to his name. The thought consoled her as violent snores drowned out the soft music from her radio.

"We're at the library!" she shouted, pulling at his arm, and he sat up with a terrifying snort.

"Good. Good." He stepped slowly out of the Toyota and stretched.

"This is the main library, and your lecture will be in that building right next door. Just walk through the front door at five fifteen and I'll meet you in the lobby. That way we'll have time to make sure the microphone works and everything is comfortable. Do you want me to come into the library with you?"

"No. Of course not." He was suddenly very brisk and she looked at him suspiciously. "I'll see you in a few hours."

"Fine."

She drove back to her office to solicit sympathy from Fran and Annie, cleared her desk, and drove home. After a quick shower, she changed into a silky lavender dress that clung to her breasts and hung softly around her legs, and was back at the lecture hall just a few minutes before Professor Austin was due.

"He's so relaxed he might just decide to forget the whole thing," she told the faculty member who planned to introduce the talk. "I'll walk over to the library. If I don't meet him on the way, I'll find him inside."

Her quarry was not en route, nor could she find him anywhere in the library. Checking her watch nervously, she persuaded a male library page to search the men's restrooms while she circled the outside of the building. There was no sign of the professor, and her stomach was in knots as she half ran back to the lecture hall. Things could hardly be worse.

"Jason!" she exclaimed in surprise as they narrowly avoided a collision. "I've lost my speaker. And," she hissed into his ear, "I think he was drunk as an owl when I picked him up."

"Can I help?"

She nodded, unable to resist another look at her watch. "He'll never be on time now, and the lecture's going to be horrible anyway." Ruffling her hair, she asked Jason, a faculty member, and a student usher to check all the buildings around the library. "I'll stay here in case he shows up," she decided, tapping her fingers frantically on a table beside her. As students began to fill the lecture hall, she closed her eyes and tried not to think about how she was going to manage the next half hour. Would Jason possibly agree to fill in for the missing speaker? Should she send everyone home?

"Here we are!" Jason's cheerful voice startled her and she opened her eyes quickly to find him and Professor Austin standing in front of her. "He was, uh, resting on one of the benches and lost track of the time. But no harm done. Should I fire a pistol or something to round up the search party?"

"No, I think everyone's back now." Lorna scowled at the redheaded professor before she waved frantically at his faculty host, who was standing in the doorway.

"We'd better get started," the faculty member said, and he and the speaker disappeared into the lecture hall.

"Coming in?" Jason asked, and Lorna shook her head.

"I can't face it. At this point I can't remember how I came to invite him here, but I just hope he was someone else's idea. In any event, I'm afraid he'll cost me my job."

Jason studied her for a moment. "My offer's still open. All my offers, in fact."

Lorna shook her head miserably.

"Whatever you say. I think I'll go on in to the lecture. I can give you a brief report later if you like."

"Only if it's good," she said, making an effort to smile.

"Can I have your autograph, Jason?" The pixie-faced young student thrust a paper and pencil in front of him, and Jason waved her away with a frown. "Not now," he said, and walked off.

"Well! I thought he was supposed to be nice," the girl said to Lorna.

"I think he values his privacy," Lorna said slowly. He had been a little unpleasant. Perhaps he was reclusive for a reason, if autograph-seekers annoyed him. But it was a little disillusioning to see him be curt. Not that she was

93

perfectly even-tempered herself, of course, but she liked to think she would be patient with her admirers if she were famous.

Glumly she perched on the edge of the table, waiting for the talk to end. Any minute now she would see the first students furtively leaving. Within an hour everyone would be wall-eyed with boredom.

She turned her head sharply as a roar of laughter came from between the double doors. The man had probably gone to sleep again, or perhaps he had knocked over the lectern. With a sigh she ran her fingers through her hair. She really should go in, but it seemed too much to face. Another wave of laughter gave her hope that perhaps all was not lost, and she tiptoed into the lecture hall, finding an aisle seat near the back.

"He's marvelous," the woman sitting next to her whispered, and in fact he was a consummate speaker, funny and informative at the same time. Lorna began to relax and enjoy herself. Next time she wouldn't be so quick to judge a visitor.

"Quite a performance," Jason said when she located him at the end, and Lorna smiled happily.

"Who would have guessed it? I wonder what he did in the library?"

"Wrote some notes and took a nap, from what he told me. Maybe I should try writing in the library instead of in Vermont."

"You haven't been able to write anything here?"

"No. Too many distractions and interruptions." He gestured as a student thrust a pen and book at him for an autograph. "It's hard for me to keep my train of thought."

"Does it annoy you when people ask for autographs?"

"I'm afraid it does," he said, opening her car door for her. "At Crowley, most people who wanted an autograph

94

have got one by now, so I'm approached less frequently than I was at first. But sometimes I feel as if I have no privacy, just because I could be bothered at any moment.

"Come here," he said suddenly as she started to get into the car, and she stepped into his arms. His embrace was warm and undemanding, and she rested her face against him, drawing comfort from the strength of his body. He stroked her back and her hair, making her body tingle expectantly. Then suddenly he released her.

"I'm expected somewhere for dinner." He studied her face for a minute. "Remember, you promised to call me as soon as you know anything. Even if it's bad news. Especially if it's bad news."

She nodded, her body tensing automatically at the thought of losing her battle. "Have a nice evening," she said tightly. "Good night."

CHAPTER SIX

Lorna and Fran were drinking coffee glumly when Annie rushed into the office, her sandals slapping firmly against her heels.

"This may be it," she said a little breathlessly, handing Lorna an envelope. She hesitated a moment, then turned to go.

"Why don't you stay," Lorna called. "After all, you know all about it."

Her heart thudding, Lorna tore awkwardly at the envelope and pulled out the letter. "It's from him," she said quietly after checking the letterhead. "I'm afraid to read it." She took a deep breath, then turned her back to the two women as she unfolded the letter with shaking hands. There were tears in her eyes, as if she already knew what the paper said, and she had to blink hard before she could read the neat type.

She read the letter twice, very carefully, then turned to face her friends. "It's all right," she said, barely able to believe it herself. "He's changed his mind." The news was beginning to penetrate, and she began to smile broadly.

"He says because the extra courses I've taken would

give me enough credits to graduate, he'll overlook the fact that I don't have a degree."

Fran snorted. "He's being very generous all of a sudden." Her own smile was wider than Lorna's, and she suddenly slapped Annie on the back. "I knew you could do it, Lorna. Let's celebrate. I think this calls for an ice cream cone."

Lorna gave her a quick hug, then absently replaced the letter in the envelope. "In about fifteen minutes, okay? I have a phone call to make."

As soon as she was alone she punched Jason's number on the phone, only to hear the harsh buzz of a busy signal. Four more tries netted the same result, and she got out her wallet with a shrug.

"My treat," she informed the other two women waiting at Annie's desk, and they walked to the campus ice cream parlor.

When the three of them returned to the administration building, replete with daiquiri chocolate chip ice cream, Lorna went straight to her office and picked up the phone. There was no answer at Jason's cottage, and she began to doubt that she would be able to reach him at all that day. What an anticlimax it would be if she ended up spending the evening alone. Somehow she had counted on being with him. She remembered the warmth of their last embrace, the gentle movement of his hands, and she tried his number again. Where was he?

Distractedly she wrote a few letters, picking up the phone every fifteen minutes and hanging up in frustration as it rang unanswered in the empty cottage. On her ninth attempt he answered the phone on the first ring, surprising her so thoroughly that she could hardly remember what she wanted to say.

"The dean's backed down," she began after an embarrassing pause, and flushed with pleasure at Jason's warm response. "I promised you a celebratory dinner," she went on. "So how about tonight?"

"I'll pick you up at seven," he said promptly. His voice dropped a little lower as he added, "I've been looking forward to spending this evening with you."

She murmured a vague reply, surprised at the sudden heat his words generated. As soon as she hung up she dialed a local French restaurant for reservations. They would have a wonderful evening, she promised herself. She pictured his face, his dark brows slightly contracted as he watched her. She remembered the evening they had spent at her house, his hands and lips moving over her body. Over and over during the afternoon she wrenched her thoughts back to the letters she was writing, only to find herself once again gazing blankly at the wall, her lips parted and her pulse racing.

Finally acknowledging she would accomplish nothing more by staying at work, she left early and hurried home to bathe and change. She was a little bit in love with Jason Coulter; that much was becoming clear. And, as a grown woman, couldn't she afford to indulge herself for a while? Her fears of becoming dependent and helpless again probably were not realistic. After all, she had handled Dean Allen without any help despite the temptation to rely on Jason. A few years ago she never would have been able to fight the battle herself.

She bathed slowly, her eyes closed as she smoothed the scented lather over her body, no longer even trying to banish thoughts of Jason. Stepping out and wrapping a towel around her, she dried her hair thoroughly, then slipped carefully into her underwear and a diagonally-striped green and white silk dress. A pair of jade and gold earrings and a matching necklace, bone sandals, and a clutch purse completed the outfit, and she began to consider her eyes. Green eyeshadow would be too obvious, she decided, limiting herself to mascara and a clear pink lipstick.

There was a new tension in her chest and stomach as she went downstairs to wait, and she could feel a pulse beating a little too rapidly in her neck. Even her breathing was noticeably quicker than usual, and she inhaled deeply to calm herself. As the minutes passed she paced restlessly around the house, checking that she had wine in the refrigerator and two clean wineglasses, flicking at occasional pieces of lint on the furniture, and glancing at her image in the mirror. At the sound of the doorbell she took another slow, deep breath, then carefully opened the door to a smiling, elegantly suited Jason bearing a magnum of champagne.

"Thank you," she said as she accepted the cold bottle. "I think I have a bucket in the kitchen."

"Could I give you a congratulatory kiss before you start searching through the cupboards?" Jason asked, his hands already on her shoulders to turn her toward him. His deep blue eyes seemed to question her as she slid her arms around his neck, and she watched them intently as they came closer, until her own eyes closed at the gentle brush of his lips. His mouth moved softly over hers until she ran her hand to the back of his head and pressed him closer. She took a long breath as his hand moved over one breast and then the other, and sighed as he pressed her tightly against him.

"We'd better have some champagne, or we'll end up missing dinner," she murmured, still clinging to him, and he embraced her strongly, his mouth against her ear.

"Whatever you say."

She pulled away reluctantly and ran her fingers quickly through her hair, feeling the heat in her cheeks. "Of course, if we open it now, most of it will go flat while we're at dinner."

He shrugged. "Maybe not. Anyway, let's live danger-ously." He gave her an enigmatic smile as he expertly loosened the cork and poured the champagne. "To vic-tory," he intoned as they raised their glasses, and Lorna frowned.

"You know, it's not as if I'd even gotten a promotion. All I did was keep my job. It's occurred to me that maybe that's not really cause for celebration."

Jason leaned comfortably against the kitchen counter. "Of course it is. You're happy that you've defended your-self successfully, and I'm happy that you're happy. You've overcome an enemy attack, after all, and without even calling on any allies. If you don't want to celebrate that, you can celebrate our second dinner together."

She smiled. "All right. Anyway, we'd better drink up and leave for L'Auberge. If we're more than five minutes late, we get drawn and quartered and, what's worse, we lose the table."

"It sounds like my kind of restaurant," he said. "Wait-ers cracking their whips over intimidated customers, a haughty maître d', and exorbitant prices."

She nodded. "Isn't that how we know we're having a nice dinner?"

He carefully recorked the champagne, nestling it into the ice-filled bucket. Then he put his arm lightly around her shoulders and she matched her steps to his as they walked out to the car.

They were rather quiet on the way to the restaurant; the only sounds were the hum of the tires on the road and the occasional rush of a car going in the opposite direc-tion. As they neared L'Auberge, Lorna began to give di-rections, her voice seeming a little loud after the silence of the ride. The restaurant was a discreet gray building that stood apart from the stores and offices on either side. The curtained windows, dimly lit from inside, offered no view of the interior, but in the entry they could see that most of the tables were already filled.

Once they were seated at a small table in the corner, conversation seemed to flow easily and Lorna relaxed a little. The tension in her stomach remained, however, and she had scant appetite for the shrimps and scallops Calvados she had ordered.

"Is it that you hate French cooking and just chose the restaurant to impress me?" he asked finally, as they sipped coffee. She shrugged.

"I'm just not very hungry tonight for some reason."

"How have you been sleeping?"

"Not very well," she admitted.

He took a last bite of chocolate mousse. "Some might attribute it to worry over your job, but I think you're falling in love." Leaning closer to her across the table, he looked at her expectantly. "I hope you haven't fallen for some stranger."

She shook her head.

He smiled and caressed her hand lightly with his fingertips. "I've had you on my mind, and I hope I've been on yours."

"I've thought about you too," she said in a choked voice, then occupied herself gratefully with the bill. As they went out into the cool night, Jason took her hand and she curled her fingers around his. In the darkness of the car she watched him as he drove, beginning to feel the breathlessness she was coming to associate with his presence.

"There's still plenty of champagne," she said huskily as he pulled into her driveway, and he nodded.

The drinks poured, she sat down near him on the print sofa and took a sip from her glass. "Still a few bubbles," she commented, watching him as he drank.

He put the glass down for a moment and took off his

jacket, draping it over the back of the sofa. His movements pulled his pale blue shirt tightly against his body, and she openly watched the play of his muscles. He loosened his dark striped tie, glancing at her for an instant, then shrugged and pulled it off and threw it over his jacket.

She studied his face—the narrow nose, the thick brows, the surprisingly full lips. She could imagine her fingers under his shirt, caressing his chest and shoulders, the thought so vivid that her skin tingled as if from real contact. As he reached for his champagne, talking quietly about a new book he had read, she slid closer to him. His voice was so rich, so soothing, it seemed to caress her, to warm her just as the pressure of his shoulder against hers generated a heat she could feel through her loose sleeve. She turned toward him a little more, bringing their knees together, but the cloth barriers between them made the contact unsatisfying. She wanted to touch him, to feel her skin warm against his, to find the places where his body was smooth and silky and the places that were rougher to her touch, partly hidden beneath a scattering of curly hair.

She could take his free hand, she thought as she watched him, without being too aggressive. With faintly trembling fingers she covered his hand with her own, relieved when he smiled, and linked their fingers together. Hesitantly she stroked the side of his hand with her thumb, wondering if he felt the same electric thrill she experienced as the sensitive ball of her thumb slid over the finely textured skin near his palm. He looked at her with his eyebrows slightly raised, a faint smile on his lips.

"What is it you want, Lorna?"

She took a deep breath. "You."

"Do you mean forever, or for the next five minutes?"

"The rest of the evening will do." She caught her lower

102

lip between her teeth as he placed his glass on the table, then turned back to her expectantly. She leaned toward him, shaking a little as she brushed her lips against his, back and forth, hardly daring to breathe. Their lips were now the only point of contact between them and all her thoughts were centered there as she gave his lower lip a tiny lick with the tip of her tongue. He caught her shoulders a little roughly and she pressed her mouth against him, no longer able to maintain her original delicacy.

She wanted him badly and she strained toward him for a moment, needing to be sure that she was not alone in her rising passion. With an effort she concentrated for an instant on unbuttoning his shirt, then slid her hand flat over his muscled chest. Immediately she felt his heartbeat, as strong and demanding as hers, and her lips curved in a faint smile as his tongue began to caress her mouth. Eagerly she explored the rises and hollows of his chest, enjoying the tickle of the crisp hair against her palm, the nubby texture of his small, hard nipples.

She felt his sharp intake of breath as she slid her hand slowly toward his waistband, and then nibbled gently at his lower lip. He pushed her back against the sofa then, sucking at her breast through the silk of her dress. The moist warmth of his mouth, the subtle pressure of his tongue through the fabric made her groan, twisting to press against him.

"Shall we go upstairs?" he asked in a low voice, and she stood up awkwardly, taking his hand.

The walk upstairs seemed endless, even with Jason close at her side, and she turned to him with a sense of relief as soon as they were through the door. Right away his fingers were at the buttons of her dress, and she stood still before him, shivering a little as he pushed the dress over her hips, his hands moving briefly down her thighs.

"Your breasts are so beautiful," he murmured as he

103

unfastened her bra and pulled the straps off her arms. "I haven't been able to get them out of my mind." He touched her nipples lightly, watching her face, and his eyes darkened as she gasped. Dizzy with longing, she put her hands on his shoulders and leaned against him lightly as his fingers moved luxuriously over her body. She had never been so feverishly ready to make love. She stepped carefully out of her shoes and over the circle of her dress on the floor and he knelt in front of her, kissing her stomach and legs as he carefully uncovered each area of skin. The pounding of her heart was so loud it nearly deafened her. Her legs were trembling, her breathing harsh by the time he pushed her onto the bed gently, removing his own clothes so quickly she barely had time to miss the warmth of his body before he was on his side next to her, his face close to hers.

He traced her collarbone with one finger as she reached out to him, her lips parted and her breasts rising and falling with her rapid breaths. "If this is not what you want, if you don't want to be here with me, say so now," he said.

"It's what I want," she whispered, pulling him toward her, and he smiled slowly, resisting the pressure of her arms.

"Not so fast." His hand moved slowly across her cheek to trace the curve of her ear. "I want to touch you and kiss you. I want you to tell me what you like, so I know how to make love to you."

She shivered helplessly as his hand moved down the curve of her waist to mold her hip, then trailed across her stomach to caress the insides of her thighs. "Tell me," he insisted, and she answered, "Yes, oh, yes," as his fingers moved and his tongue circled her nipple.

He seemed to know her body better than she did herself, and she clung to him helplessly as he kissed and stroked her inner thighs. His warm breath tortured her, his tongue and fingers aroused her beyond endurance, and she tangled her fingers in his hair. "Please, Jason."

She bit his shoulder when he entered her at last, and caressed his back with trembling hands. She couldn't get enough of him. She kissed the hollow of his collarbone, his neck, then cried out as her nerve endings exploded again and again into exquisite showers of sensation. He gave a long shuddering sigh and kissed her fiercely, and she held him tightly against her.

Ignoring an insane desire to tell him that she loved him, she stroked his neck and shoulders as he relaxed against her. As he rolled to his side she turned to move with him, looking into his smiling face. His eyes were very blue, his dark hair rumpled on his forehead. She lay quietly in his arms, enjoying his gentle massage of the muscles of her back. She'd never even imagined lovemaking like this, so tender and still so passionate. She'd never thought she could lose herself so completely.

"I've imagined this night many times," he murmured, one hand moving to caress her hip. "But the reality far exceeds my fantasies."

"I'm glad," she said almost inaudibly, suddenly feeling a little shy. Somehow she'd just assumed it had been the same for him as for her, but of course she couldn't be sure. He'd been with dozens of women, probably, and maybe he'd expected something different from her, something more.

"You've been so afraid of this, but tonight I don't think you held anything back. Are you convinced now that it's safe to be a little vulnerable?"

Lorna gazed up at the ceiling. She was more than a little vulnerable now. She'd pretended to herself, and maybe to him, that she could control her feelings, give in to her physical attraction without involving her emotions. She couldn't fool herself anymore, but with any luck she'd keep him from guessing the depth of feeling she'd discovered this evening.

"This is not safe at all," she said finally, "but it's definitely worth the risk."

Jason laughed. "I suppose I'll have to be satisfied with that for the time being."

She pulled away to look at him and he ran one finger lightly down her nose.

"Would you like a little more champagne?" he asked, and she nodded.

"I'll get it," she said. "I'm starving all of a sudden, and I think I'll bring up some cheese and crackers."

He ran his hand down her back and over her buttocks as she stood up. "That's what happens when you don't eat your dinner."

It felt perfectly natural to be naked in bed with him, chatting about cheese and crackers, she thought as she fixed a tray to carry back upstairs. She'd have to remember that this would all have to come to an end. She climbed the stairs slowly, balancing the champagne bottle, and gave an involuntary smile at the sight of him stretched out between the sheets. He was so handsome, so gentle, altogether too wonderful to resist.

"I never thought you were the kind of woman who would eat crackers in bed," he remarked as they sat against her pillows a few minutes later.

"Well, it's my bed, after all."

"Perfectly correct. If you enjoy rolling around in cracker crumbs all night, who am I to pass judgment on you?"

She shrugged grandly, spilling several ounces of champagne down her naked chest.

"Allow me," he murmured as she looked around for a tissue, and bent to lick the wine from her skin. She

106

stroked him, enjoying the breadth of his shoulders, the hard muscles of his arms, then gradually moved her hands lower on his body. As he lifted his head to kiss her she caressed his waist, running her hand lightly down to the back of his thighs. His body was very different from hers, tight and hard against her softness, and to her surprise she wanted him again, even more than she had before. She explored his mouth with her tongue, her hips moving urgently against him, and she sighed with satisfaction as she felt his arousal.

He pulled her over him and she resumed their kiss, supremely confident in her newfound knowledge of him. Their lovemaking was slower this time as they unhurriedly explored each other's responses, and she felt suspended in time, utterly absorbed in the union of their bodies.

"I'm going to make love to you for a long, long time," Jason said thickly, and she bit his lip lightly. With one hand she caressed the inside of his thigh, and he groaned. "Let's roll over," he said softly, and soon she was clutching him feverishly. All her restraint had gone, and she shuddered and sobbed in his embrace, her back arched, her head thrown back as tiny electric currents traveled up and down her body. She became overwhelmingly tender as she felt his release, and stroked his hair gently. She felt closer to him than she had ever thought possible. She couldn't bear the thought of his leaving.

"Will you stay with me tonight?" she asked.

"If that's what you want." He brushed a lock of hair out of her eyes and she nestled against him contentedly, determined to take each day as it came.

She awoke to the smell of coffee and quickly slipped a caftan over her head. As she padded down the stairs she heard Jason whistling, and stopped on the bottom step with a sudden sense of panic. She was in some ways a good cook, but somehow at breakfast her skills evaporated. As Ward had often pointed out, the toast she made was invariably too brown or too white, the egg too hard or too soft, the coffee too strong or too weak. She would have to do better with Jason.

"I'm sorry I slept so late," she said, pausing at the kitchen door. "I'll fix breakfast as soon as I've taken a shower."

Jason was sitting on one of her high stools, fully dressed, apparently waiting for the coffeemaker to finish.

"Or would you rather I cooked it right away?" She stood in front of him, her hands clenched in the pockets of her caftan and he stepped down easily from the stool.

"I fully intended to bring you breakfast in bed," he said. "But since you're awake . . ."

He pulled her close and she leaned stiffly against him, her hands still in her pockets. She tried to take in what he had said. No one had ever brought her breakfast in bed— or anywhere else for that matter. She relaxed gradually as his hands smoothed her hair.

"Is it important to you to cook breakfast? Is that the problem?" he asked, tilting her head up to kiss her lightly on the lips.

She laughed suddenly and put her arms around him, snuggling against him. "No, actually I really don't want to cook breakfast at all."

"Fine. You shower and I'll cook. But we'll have to hurry. I still have to shave and change clothes before my office hours start."

She stepped back quickly, looking into his eyes for a moment before she ran lightly upstairs. He was nothing like Ward, she told herself as the shower pummeled her shoulders. She'd have to stop expecting him to hurt her in the same ways. Jason was a sensitive, tender lover, and he could cook too. She smiled as she rinsed her hair. She was lucky to have made love with Jason, lucky to have known him at all. From now on she would try to see him as he really was.

She dried her hair and dressed rapidly in a gray dress with white trim, buckled her soft white leather belt, and ran downstairs in her stocking feet.

"Am I too late?" she asked, seeing the plates already on the snack bar.

"I just served it," he assured her, and she sat down eagerly.

"A western omelette?" She cut into the perfect half circle. "And the bacon looks beautiful too. My cooking never would have lived up to your standards."

He stood behind her, his arms crossed under her breasts, and kissed the side of her neck just under her ear. "I don't have any standards for you to meet. I just want you to relax and let things happen."

She was silent as he sat back on his stool. "I don't know," she said finally, "if I can just let this happen."

"What are you afraid of?" he asked, finishing his last piece of bacon.

She felt her lip begin to tremble and looked away from his serious face. "I guess I'm afraid you'll break my heart."

"I wouldn't want to do that," he said steadily. "We both know I'm here only for the summer. But if things work out, I could come back for visits, or you could visit me. Let's just take things one step at a time. We still have a lot to learn about each other."

He stood up and held out his arms, and she stepped into them immediately, finding comfort in the strength of his embrace.

"I don't want to pressure you if you need some time to yourself right now," he said. "Why don't you call me

109

when you're ready. It can be this afternoon, next week, or two weeks from now. Whatever seems right to you."

"Okay." She swallowed painfully. It would be easier somehow if he tried to pressure her, persuade her to give in to his desires. It would make her more sure that he wanted her. This way she would have to expose herself completely, admit to him and to herself how much she wanted him. She didn't know at that moment what she would do.

"I have to run." He cupped her chin with one hand and kissed her very softly. "Don't forget to call."

He seemed always to be saying that to her. She felt her smile begin to tremble and turned away quickly. He kissed her lightly on the temple, then was gone.

After she heard his car start up she washed the breakfast dishes. She drove to the campus in a daze, and entered her office just as Fran walked by.

"You don't look as exuberant as I would have expected," Fran said. "After all, you've just won a great moral victory, but for some reason you're very pensive."

Lorna thought for a few seconds. "I suppose I'm a little let down after being keyed up for so long."

She was hardly able to tell Fran that she was reliving the previous night, remembering every touch, every whispered endearment. More than anything she wanted to call him at that very moment, to be reassured by his deep voice. She wanted to know when she could see him again, when she could lie naked in his arms.

She looked out over the courtyard, remembering the day she had met Jason and they had stood together at the window. Even that first telephone conversation had told her that she would find him powerfully attractive. And now . . . She turned briskly away from the window and sat down at her desk. She forbade herself to worry over her relationship with Jason. After she made up her mind to relax and take one step at a time, she began to work on the day's tasks.

"Yes, Mr. Grant, I do understand," she was saying for the fifth time when Annie came to lean against the door-jamb, signaling urgently that there was another call. "I'll do my best," Lorna promised hastily, and hung up.

"President Arnold's on the other line," Annie said, and Lorna obediently punched the glowing button on her telephone.

Could Jason have been behind the call, she wondered a few moments later as she replaced the receiver. Why else would the president have made a point of reassuring her about her job? But Jason had promised to stay out of it, and she would have to trust him.

Reaching in her file drawer for her list of local motels, she crossed off the one that had housed the Woebegone Werewolves, then turned back to the beginning of the list.

"What's up?"

Lorna looked up in surprise to see her sister just outside the door, her blond hair newly cut and curled.

"I never see you anymore, so I thought I'd take a chance and drop in."

Lorna waved at the black chair. "Sit down. You look terrific. Is that a new dress?"

Beth nodded. "I'm tired of being a dowdy old matron, and I think maybe Phil is tired of it, too. So I just got made over. But I was afraid to go home and face everyone without getting someone else's opinion first. Do you really like it?"

Lorna took in the softly curled hair, skillful makeup, and the tailored dress that accented her sister's long legs and narrow waist. "I think this is the first time anyone in the family has looked really sophisticated instead of just clean and healthy. If you don't mind being imitated, I might even try it myself."

Beth turned a little pink. "Be my guest. I suppose you need to get back to work now."

Lorna sighed. "Coleman Grant has informed me he can come to Crowley only if his motel room is pink."

"Pink?" Beth's eyebrows climbed into her new curls.

"Pink induces tranquil creativity," Lorna informed her, mimicking the author's careful enunciation. "Blue and green, more commonly used in motels, are conducive to lethargy and depression. Anyway, that's his theory and he's standing behind it. So I'm calling every motel in town to see if they have any pink rooms."

Beth stood up to go. "If worse comes to worst, he can always stay in Katy's room. It's pink with white ruffles everywhere."

"If I thought you were serious, I might take you up on that." Lorna marked the next motel on her list with her pencil. "Say hello to Phil for me. I know he'll love everything once he gets used to it."

"Right. In another three or four years." Beth gathered up her purse. "Anything new with your job?"

Lorna gasped. "I forgot to tell you! Everything's fine now, thank you."

"Nothing else new?" Beth looked at her closely.

"Not a thing," Lorna lied cheerfully, and turned back to the telephone. If she told her sister what had happened between her and Jason, Beth would probably assume that a marriage was imminent. And, of course, there was no chance of that.

She took a deep breath. No matter how much she longed to hear his voice, she couldn't call Jason until she was in control of her feelings. Today she felt helpless and dependent, badly wanting reassurance that he cared for her. Somehow she'd have to subdue those wishes and make sure she could meet him as an equal.

CHAPTER SEVEN

She stared at the beige telephone as if it were an alien invader sitting on her kitchen snack bar. "Face it," she told herself bitterly. "You're dying to call him. If you weren't such a coward, you'd have done it days ago."

She walked absently to the refrigerator and peered inside. Food didn't seem to be the answer, and she closed the door abruptly, deciding to make some camomile tea. She turned over a record while the water came to a boil, then stood again by the phone. Flipping open her address book to the number of Jason's cottage, she took a deep breath and reached for the receiver just as the teakettle began to whistle.

With a muttered curse she splashed some boiling water into the small brown teapot and went back to the phone, dialing quickly before she could change her mind. There was no answer.

"So much for that." She shoved the telephone savagely down on the white counter and poured a cup of the pale yellow tea. Shrugging, she took a tiny sip and picked up the phone again.

"Beth," she said a few seconds later. "Where did you get your hair done?"

113

"At Lizbett's," Beth replied. "Are you really going to do it?"

"I guess. I've been feeling so *blah* lately, I need a change."

"How about one of those singles cruises?" Beth said. "Or a tour of some kind? I bet a little romance would solve the problem."

Lorna snorted. "Not a chance. I'll settle for a new haircut. How did Phil take yours, by the way?"

Beth's voice dropped to a whisper. "It really shook him at first. I almost went back to tell them to put everything back the way they had found it. But now I think he's beginning to like it."

"Good."

"It's more fun, you know, when you're doing it for someone else. Won't you feel let down if you get all beautified and then just go home with no one there to admire you?"

Lorna shook her head. "You've got a one-track mind."

"Well, I was thinking. If you wanted, I could have one of Phil's friends over for dinner. . . ."

"No, thanks. I'll survive."

She hung up soon after that, and went upstairs to get ready for bed. Her image in the mirror was so familiar, it was difficult to imagine it with curly hair or more sophisticated makeup. Would she turn out looking like Beth, or like a completely new person? *You'd be doing it only to impress Jason Coulter,* a small voice told her just as she was falling asleep, and she knew she would never see the inside of Lizbett's.

"I got tired of sitting by the telephone," Jason's voice sounded as she was searching through her desk drawer, and she looked up, feeling an idiotic smile spread across her face.

"You weren't sitting by the phone last night."

He grinned and turned to click her office door shut. "So you did call."

"Just that one time," she said quickly as he came to stand behind her chair, his thumbs massaging her shoulders.

"Relax," he said softly. "Just let your muscles go." Slowly she allowed her head to rest against his chest as his fingers dug almost painfully into her back. "What I'd like to do tonight is take you out to dinner and then take you home and make love to you."

She sat up involuntarily and he stopped his massage, allowing his hands to rest on her shoulders.

"Come and sit down," she said a little breathlessly. "I can't talk to you when you're standing behind me."

"Okay." He left her to sit on the other side of the desk.

"I have to listen to a zitherist tonight."

"How exotic. Are you a zither fan?"

"No, but who knows? Someday someone might need a zither player. If I go tonight, I'll be able to find out something about this one anyway. He's a guest of the history department over at the university, and I don't know yet how they found him."

"Well, may I come along?"

"Of course." Lorna smiled. "It will surely beat the Werewolves' concert. And it's even indoors. Why don't I stop by for you a little before eight."

He made a sudden gesture, as if she had surprised him, then spread his hands. "Fine."

She was still smiling as he left, and she turned her chair away from the door to hide her expression from passersby. If she was going to be moonstruck, at least she could do it in privacy. She took a deep breath to slow the lurching of her heart and dreamily picked up a pencil, wondering what she would wear that night.

"Stay here with me tonight," he murmured into her hair as she lay beside him in the bedroom of his cottage, her skin still faintly damp from their recent lovemaking. "I'll wake you up early enough to get home and change."

She bit her lip, looking around the dimly lit room. "I don't want to leave, but I don't know."

He propped himself up on one elbow to look at her. "Are you afraid someone will see your car outside?"

"No."

"What then?"

"I feel as if I'm getting too attached to you. I guess I'm trying to preserve some distance between us."

"And by driving home tonight you'll make that happen?" Jason's voice was very tender.

"I don't know." She felt the first stirrings of anxiety and rolled out of bed. "I guess I'll take a shower."

"May I join you?"

"Of course. If you really want to shower in the middle of the night."

He stood behind her, his arms around her waist. "To be with you." His hand moved down her thigh and she stepped away to walk to the bathroom.

He opened the glass shower door and turned on the hot water while she stood a little awkwardly in the chilly bathroom, her arms folded across his chest.

"Here," he said with a smile, "let me keep you warm." He pulled her against him, wrapping his arms tightly around her, and unwillingly she felt her body's automatic response to his embrace. She lifted her face and he lowered his lips to hers, his mouth soft and caressing. As waves of steam enveloped them, she sighed and slowly pulled away.

"I think the water's hot now," she said, and he laughed softly.

"I hadn't noticed." He lowered the temperature of the water, then took her hand and led her into the blue-tiled shower stall, clicking the door shut behind them.

It was like a tiny private world, she thought while he worked the soap into a lather—tropical and pleasantly scented. He put the soap back in its dish and took her hand again, carefully lathering each finger before drawing soapy circles on her palm. Delicately his fingers moved up her lower arm, spreading foam with their motion, one hand on the sensitive underside of her arm, the other stroking the top. He took the soap again for a few moments, then lovingly applied himself to her upper arm and shoulder. Her skin was beginning to tingle pleasantly and she closed her eyes dreamily when he began soaping her left hand.

Again he moved slowly up to her shoulder, then knelt to lather her feet. She leaned back slightly against the shower wall, already anticipating his touch on her thighs and the delicate strokes at her feminine recesses. The water beat gently on her chest and stomach as she stood, breathing quickly while his hands made leisurely journeys up and down the slippery skin.

She opened her eyes a slit and saw that he was looking up at her, the water running into his eyes. Softly, one foamy hand began to travel back and forth between her breasts. She closed her eyes again and sought more support from the wall as his other hand played with the blond curls below her stomach. His delicate caresses made her knees weak, and she touched his shoulders, smiling down at him. "It's my turn now." She had no more thoughts of going home.

The soap lathered quickly in the soft water and she spread the rich suds over his chest, enjoying the varying textures of skin and curly hair against her palm. The hair on his head was very wet and dark, plastered against his

117

skull. It made his nose seem sharper, his eyes more deep-set, and he looked wonderfully handsome.

She began soaping lower, circling his navel, and he gripped her hips lightly to pull her toward him. She nuzzled his shoulder happily, feeling him hard against her stomach, then lifted her head to kiss him deeply.

"Maybe we could find someplace a little more comfortable than the shower," she murmured against his cheek, and his hands tightened on her buttocks.

"There's a very soft rug in here," he said, stroking her thighs, "and the room is nice and warm now."

Lorna nibbled at his earlobe. "What are we waiting for?"

Within seconds they were together on the rug, their skin wet, their bodies intimately joined. Every time they made love, as they grew more familiar with each other, the experience for Lorna was more profound. She was no longer aware of the physical details, of the sounds she made. Now she didn't feel even a faint hint of uncertainty. When her arms were around him like this, when she was warmed by the heat of their bodies, nothing seemed to matter but their closeness. Jason had never said he loved her, or even that he cared for her, but during these moments his tenderness, his sensitivity, and the urgency of his response to her made words unnecessary.

"I didn't know I could feel like this," she whispered later as they lay cuddled together in bed. "It makes me a little nervous." Her earlier confidence was dissolving, and she was again aware that she was more deeply involved with Jason than was safe.

He pulled her a little closer. "There's lots of time for you to learn to trust what we have together."

"We have the summer, at least," she murmured, burying her face in his shoulder, and drifting off into sleep.

"What time is it?" she asked sharply the next morning as his hand moved slowly down her spine.

"It's not quite as early as I had hoped," he said softly. "If you insist on being punctual, I'm afraid I'd better cook breakfast while you shower and dress."

"Okay." She trotted quickly to the shower, shivering in the morning air, and caught a glimpse of herself in the mirror, her flushed cheeks and disheveled hair giving her an incongruously childlike appearance. She showered quickly and dressed in record time in the slacks she had worn to the zither concert.

"I think I'll just grab some coffee and toast and run home to change," she told Jason, kissing him lightly on the cheek.

"Are you always so prickly in the morning?" he asked, handing her a cup. When she didn't reply, he went on. "I hope in time you'll relax a little. I always seem to be saying that to you."

She winced as she gulped the hot coffee. "I'm trying."

Picking up her purse, she planted a noisy kiss on his cheek, then hugged him tightly. He was so dear to her, his embrace so comforting, that she didn't want to let go.

"Lorna, I have something on tonight, but I'll call you tomorrow, okay?"

She rubbed her cheek against the soft velour of his bathrobe. "Fine." She sighed. "I really should go."

"Well, put your purse down for a minute and give me a real kiss."

The purse hit the floor with a soft thud and she raised her arms to link them around his neck while her lips moved softly over his. It was a slow, gentle kiss, and she gave a tiny smile as she felt his arousal. Pulling away slightly, she kissed his cheek, leaning back a little against his encircling arms. "If I don't leave now," she breathed into his ear, "I may be here all morning."

119

He pulled her abruptly closer. "That sounds like a delightful idea."

She laughed, shaking her head. "Only if I want to be unemployed."

"I don't suppose you'd consider calling in sick." He tilted her chin to look at her and she studied his smile, wondering if he was at all serious.

"I'd better not." She kissed him again, pressing hard against his lips, then backed slowly away. He caught her hand and they stood there for a minute, smiling at each other.

"I'd walk you to the car," he said, "but in my present condition I don't think it would do much for your reputation."

Lorna laughed. "I don't know. It might do wonders for my staid image." She kissed him one last time. "You'll call tomorrow?"

"I will."

She picked up her purse, squeezed his hand for an instant, then hurried out to her car. It would be a long twenty-four hours or more before she talked to him again, and it would be very hard for her to be alone tonight. Yet, she knew she couldn't afford to get any more deeply involved, and this was an opportunity to prove to herself that she was still independent. Maybe she would call one of her friends and go to a movie.

Once at her house, she changed quickly into a khaki skirt and plaid blouse and trotted back to the car.

"Well, you seem particularly contented today," Fran remarked as they stood by the coffee machine. "There's something a little different about you." She studied Lorna so closely that she began to fidget a little. "You're not pregnant, are you?" she hissed, and Lorna laughed, a little relieved.

"No fear. I don't take those kind of chances."

"Well," Fran replied smugly, "if you're not pregnant, you must be in love. Do I get three guesses?"

Lorna looked quickly over her shoulder. "You're embarrassing me, and someone might hear you."

"Oh, I can be discreet." At Lorna's look of disbelief, Fran added, "Not about work, but about personal things. At least I think I could if I really tried. Anyway, if his initials are J.C. and he writes poetry, I wish I could take your place." She sighed deeply. "Some women have all the luck. But you deserve it, after being married to that SOB."

Lorna jerked in surprise and spilled a few drops of coffee on the carpet. "Is that really what you thought of Ward?"

Fran shrugged. "I think most of us felt that way. But I didn't mean to be rude about it. Just enjoy what you've got."

Lorna took a deep breath. "I'm trying."

Back at her desk, Lorna flipped idly through a stack of papers. Things had finally slowed down a little. But she still needed to book a room for Coleman Grant. She went out to Annie's desk with her list.

"We need a pink motel room for Coleman Grant. Just take my word for it," she said firmly as Annie began an incredulous protest. "We need it. So you start on this list at the S's, and work back as far as E. I'll be going from T to Z and I've already called from A to E. If we fail, he'll have to stay in my niece's room, and I'm not sure any of us is ready for that."

Three hours later, neither she nor Annie had any success. "I've got only five more places on my list," Lorna reported.

"I just made my last call," Annie told her. "I guess it doesn't look good."

121

"Well, we can't give up until we've done it all." Lorna resolutely put the receiver to her ear.

A few minutes later she called through the door. "I did it! I found a bridal suite with pink brocade drapes, wallpaper with pink hearts, *and* a heart-shaped pink tub."

"Congratulations." Annie sounded as if she were restraining hysterical laughter.

"Now I have the pleasure of telephoning Coleman Grant again." Lorna sighed and picked up the receiver. "Sometimes I feel as if I were born with a telephone receiver attached to my ear."

Her call completed, she still felt on edge, and she decided to walk to the coffee house for some iced tea. When she returned to her desk, she picked up a small square envelope with her name printed firmly across the front. Some kind of invitation, she thought briefly, then flushed hotly as she unfolded the note.

"Your breasts are as soft as magnolia petals," she read unbelievingly, and quickly refolded the paper, knowing that a foolish grin was spreading across her face. So he had been thinking of her after all. With renewed energy she returned to her work, resolving to spend the evening quietly and uncomplainingly alone.

As he had promised, Jason called her at work the next morning.

"Thank you for the note," Lorna said.

"You sound a little uncertain. Did you object to the topic, the metaphor, or the method of delivery?"

"The topic, I suppose."

"No more breast notes." He sighed heavily. "I'll just have to move on to other areas, I guess."

She laughed. "You mean like eyes, hair, and lips?"

"Too traditional. That's already been done. No, I can see myself discovering new vistas of poetic expression," he said suggestively.

"On second thought, breasts are a fine topic."

"I'm glad we agree."

Lorna hesitated. "Would you like to have dinner together tonight?"

"That sounds good." He was silent for a moment. "How about if I pick you up at your office and we can go out for a Chinese dinner?"

"Fine."

She was quite exhilarated after they had hung up. She had never taken the initiative with a man before, but it was a good feeling, particularly when her overtures were successful. Jason seemed perfectly at ease with her occasional bouts of self-assertion. More so than she was, probably. She cleared her desk easily and spent a little time combing her hair and renewing her lipstick before he arrived.

She was rather quiet during dinner, enjoying Jason's tales of his adventures in getting his house built and furnished. He had had to bribe people outrageously to convince them to drive their delivery trucks over the rough roads to his house, and on occasion had been forced to take the wheel himself. Living in a remote area obviously presented a number of problems Lorna had never even considered.

She opened her fortune cookie. "Soon you will be near the water," it read, and she showed it to Jason.

"Cookies never lie. I'm going to visit my friends in Carmel this weekend, and I was planning to ask you to come along."

Lorna hesitated. "You mean spend the night?"

"We'd probably drive down Saturday and come back the next day."

"If your friends won't mind," she said slowly.

"They'll enjoy meeting you, and they're not going to be

concerned about our sleeping arrangements, if that's what's bothering you."

She nodded. "Okay. I love the coast."

He drove her home in silence, then turned to her with a grin. "Your car's still on the campus, isn't it? If you let me spend the night, I'll drive you to work in the morning."

"It's not necessary to bribe me." She pulled him close and kissed him softly on the lips. "I would have asked you to stay anyway."

"I'm going to Carmel with Jason Coulter," she told Beth abruptly the next afternoon, "so I won't be around this weekend."

"Wonderful." Beth's voice was unenthusiastic, and Lorna wished they were face-to-face instead of talking on the telephone.

"You don't approve?"

"I just don't want you to get hurt. Are you in love with him?"

"Neither of us has even mentioned the word." Lorna tapped her eraser on her desk.

"Well, have a good time. I hope it's not too foggy."

Lorna packed carefully, uncertain how to approach the weekend. She selected a modest silk nightgown and a blue velour robe to ensure that she wouldn't be embarrassed, some casual clothes for the beach, and a dress in case they went out to dinner. "Of course," she told herself scornfully, "you could also pack a dress for shopping in Carmel, another one for wine-tasting, and something in case we *don't* go out for dinner."

Still, her suitcase was respectably small. She examined her beige slacks and striped blouse critically in the mirror before carrying her sweater and suitcase downstairs. She heard Jason's car soon after that, and her heart lifted at the sight of him on her doorstep, handsome as always in khaki slacks and a blue knit shirt. They exchanged a warm, lingering kiss until Lorna pulled away slightly, her heart hammering against her ribs.

"Do you want a cup of coffee or something before we leave?" she asked huskily, trailing a finger behind his ear to the soft hairs at the back of his neck.

He smiled and closed the door quietly behind him. "Or something," he murmured, his lips moving against her throat. "We have lots of time."

She drew a long, trembling breath as his hands cupped her buttocks, pressing her against him as his tongue moved delicately between her lips. With a smile he picked her up easily and carried her to the sofa, where he laid her down softly and knelt beside her on the floor. Deftly he removed her clothes, his caressing lips and tongue distracting her so thoroughly that she was barely aware that she was being gently undressed.

She reached for him with a moan as his lips moved warmly down her stomach, and was startled to feel the cloth of his shirt. "You're all covered up," she complained, fumbling awkwardly with his buttons. Suddenly she felt herself losing control as his knowing hands found the center of the sensations that radiated up and down her body. She sobbed his name, clutching his shirt in her fists, then released him reluctantly to allow him to strip off his clothes.

"It just keeps getting more wonderful," she murmured brokenly as their bodies moved together.

"I know. I know," he whispered as she thrust upward to shatter his control, her hands seeking out the places that would arouse him the most.

They lay quietly for a while, Jason's arms partially supporting his weight as she lay contented beneath him, her fingers tracing his biceps, then moving to his neck.

125

Unexpectedly he gave her a gentle slap on the thigh. "Let's get going," he said as he stood up.

"And I thought the fun was just beginning," Lorna complained, getting up and smoothing down her hair.

Jason's eyes narrowed. "Don't ask for more than you can handle." He bent to kiss her breasts, his mouth sliding easily over the faintly damp skin, and Lorna shook her head, hugging him hard.

"I take it back," she laughed.

"That was mostly bluff anyway." He squeezed her so tightly that she gasped. "Although if you'd care to wait around a few minutes . . ."

"I suppose we'd better go."

"Let's drive down the coast and have lunch in Monterey," he said later as they put her suitcase in the car. "Being near the ocean is a treat for those of us from landlocked states."

"Fine." She settled comfortably into the front seat, her face turned away from him to look out the window as an indefinable sadness crept over her. As the tree-covered slopes of the Santa Cruz Mountains were replaced by inland fields of artichoke plants, she asked herself what she would do at the end of the summer. Her feelings for Jason grew stronger every day, and she was nearly helpless in the face of his sexual power over her. His life in California was so different from his life in Vermont. In some ways, she hardly knew him at all. Just as one should expect in a summer fling, she reminded herself cruelly. The limits to the relationship were obvious, and she should learn to accept them.

"You're very pensive," Jason said as he parked near the wharf in Monterey. "Are you uncomfortable about this weekend?"

"No." Lorna forced a smile. "I was just trying to think some things through."

126

"I'll be glad to hear your thoughts when you're ready to tell me." He took her hand and they walked down the wharf, stopping at a small Mediterranean restaurant that had several empty tables with a view of the bay.

The table next to them was made up of a three-generation Italian family, obviously having a wonderful time, and Jason smiled a little sadly at the antics of the three small children.

"Do you ever miss that?"

"I'm not sure. When I was married I was afraid to have children. Ward was such a perfectionist, I was sure he'd never be pleased with them, that he'd destroy their self-confidence."

Jason took her hand across the table. "Did he destroy yours?"

"I must not have had much to begin with, or I wouldn't have let him intimidate me so much. And maybe I'm being unfair to him. He's as hard on himself as he is on everyone else. Maybe having a child would have softened him."

"Did he want children?"

"Not really. He knew that eventually he'd have two children, a boy and a girl, because that's what one does. But I don't think he'd thought much about it beyond that. It seemed as if we had plenty of time."

"Sometimes I wish I'd remarried and had kids," Jason said slowly. "And I wonder if it's too late."

"I know. Sometimes I feel as if that's all passing me by too. But I'm sure it's not too late for anything you really want." She squeezed his hand.

"Maybe not." He pulled his hand away to butter his roll.

After lunch they strolled around the wharf, enjoying the sea smell of the cool, damp breeze, until Jason checked his watch. "We might as well drive on to Tom and Miriam's, unless there's something else you want to see here."

Lorna shook her head. Her apprehension about being introduced to Jason's friends was increasing, and she wasn't inclined to delay the meeting.

"Mesembryanthemum," Jason murmured as they drove through Pacific Grove. "I'd love to write a poem about all those hot pink flowers. But mesembryanthemum is too much of a tongue-twister."

Lorna squinted at the plants covering much of the ground that sloped to the ocean. "I don't believe it's called that at all. That's just plain old ice plant."

"Trust me." He put his hand on her knee. "Speaking of which, I'm not bringing you down here to see if my friends approve of you. I'm bringing you so that you can enjoy each other. There's nothing to be nervous about."

"Okay." She tried to relax back against her seat.

"They live right in the village, in a tan adobe house next to one of those horrible Hansel and Gretel houses. Personally, I'd hate to live in a place that's so artsy that nobody even numbers their houses."

"Is that it?" Lorna pointed to a rather square tan house set far back in the trees. "The mailbox says Berwick."

"This is it." He turned into the graveled drive and parked in front of a small adobe garage.

As they got out of the car, two people came outside the door. Both were unusually tall, well over six feet, and solidly built. The man's dark gray hair and hawklike face made him seem rather formidable. The woman was somewhat less intimidating, primarily because her soft white hair flew in wisps around her strongly featured face and gave it a hint of grandmotherly softness. Lorna soon found herself in the bright yellow kitchen with Miriam making herb tea while Jason and Tom went outside to examine a tree that Tom had decided to remove.

"I thought we'd go out to dinner," Miriam said, "so we'll just spend a quiet afternoon, unless you're interested in the craft shops."

Lorna shook her head. "I always end up buying things I don't need, and then they look awful when I get them home. I'd rather take a walk to the beach."

"My feelings exactly." Miriam gestured at several framed dried flower arrangements that decorated one wall. "Have you known Jason long?"

Lorna sank down on a cane-backed chair. "Several weeks, I guess."

"I don't know how much you know about his past . . ." Miriam hesitated, and Lorna realized that she knew almost nothing specific beyond what had been written in the newspaper.

"Not very much."

"Well, Tom would be furious at me for meddling, and I must admit that he's usually right." Miriam carefully poured tea into two earthenware mugs. "But Jason has had a tendency to drift in and out of relationships ever since I've known him."

Lorna traced the handle of her mug with one finger. "You're saying I shouldn't get too serious about Jason." She looked across the table into Miriam's worried brown eyes.

"I'd be a little careful if I were you. I gather Jason never got over his wife." Miriam's voice was so low Lorna could barely hear it. She disliked the feeling that she was listening to gossip about Jason behind his back, but at the same time she wanted to learn more about him, more than he had told her.

"What was she like?"

Miriam shook her head. "We met him long after the

divorce, so I never knew her. But we've seen him with several different women over the years, and there were more whom we never met. My own feeling is that if Jason wanted to settle down, he would have done so long ago."

Lorna sighed. "You're probably right."

Exactly how many other women had Miriam and Tom met, she wondered. Jason had never talked about his marriage, much less more recent relationships. She wrapped her hand around her mug to see if the tea was still too hot to drink, responding absently to Miriam's questions about her job while part of her mind continued to worry about Jason.

The afternoon passed pleasantly as the four of them wandered casually in and out of the house and along the road that led to the beach. Lorna had an opportunity to get acquainted with both Tom and Miriam, but somehow saw little of Jason. They dressed for dinner separately, and even at the cozy table at the Pump House most of Jason's conversation was directed at Miriam.

After a tiny glass of cognac in the candlelit living room, Lorna said good night and went into the bedroom she was sharing with Jason. Hurriedly she unzipped her taupe and white striped broadcloth dress and untied the brown silk bow at the neck. Stripping off her clothes, she pulled on her nightgown and got into the queen-size bed, leaving a small lamp on for Jason. She almost hoped she would be asleep before he came to bed, but in fact he opened the bedroom door just a few minutes later.

"I didn't want you to feel neglected," he said with a grin, but Lorna didn't reply. She had felt neglected, actually, but somehow she didn't want the kind of attention he was offering now. She glanced away as he pulled off his clothes, folding them neatly on a chair, and she lay still as he climbed into bed.

"What's this? A nightgown?" His fingers ran down the thin straps. "Are you trying to tell me something?"

"I guess I am," Lorna whispered.

"If you're uncomfortable here, I don't want to pressure you." He pulled her close to him, nestling her head against his chest. "Just let me hold you," he said, and gradually she relaxed while his slow, steady heartbeat soothed and reassured her. His arms were warm around her and she lay very still, thinking.

"How many women have you made love to?" she asked after a time, and there was no response. She lifted her head slightly and saw that he was asleep.

Sunday was foggy, and Tom and Miriam showed little enthusiasm for a walk to the beach. After a pancake breakfast they read the paper and drank coffee for a while, then Miriam took Lorna to her small studio in back of the house. Lorna stayed there by herself to explore among the stacks of paintings. Miriam's most recent works all showed a turbulent ocean under overcast skies, but there were earlier pictures of pelicans, seals, and one of cypress trees on a cliff.

The door opened with a tiny scraping sound and she turned to see Jason standing there, Lorna's down jacket in his hand.

"I thought you'd gotten lost in the fog and couldn't find your way back to the house," he said.

"Have I been in here that long?"

"Not really." He put the jacket down on a paint-stained wooden table. "But I missed you."

He held out his arms and she went to him, Miriam's words echoing in her head. She nestled her face against his soft wool sweater for a moment, then looked up at him, returning his smile in spite of her worry. He kissed her, his hands moving down her back to cup her buttocks and press her against him.

As they stood there, their lips moving tenderly against each other, he ran his hands down the back of her blue-jeaned thighs, his caressing thumbs hinting at further intimacies, exciting her even through the cloth. She moaned and he pressed her more tightly against him.

"I don't suppose Miriam has a nice soft mattress tucked away in her studio," he said.

Lorna smiled up at him again. "Not that I've noticed."

He kissed her, his lips quick and firm. "Actually, I came out to see if you'd like to drive out to the point and look for seals. Miriam is planning lunch for one o'clock, so we have lots of time."

Lorna put on her jacket. "I'm sure it's too foggy to see anything, but I'm game."

The fog beaded heavily on the windshield as they drove back around the coast, and they had the rocky beach to themselves. They climbed out on the slippery rocks very carefully and stood on an outcropping, the waves breaking just beneath them.

"I think the tide's coming in," Lorna laughed as a spray of saltwater made them retreat several feet. "Let's make sure we don't get trapped out here."

Jason put an arm around her. "Why? I think it would be rather romantic, huddled together on a cold, wet spur of rock. Or better yet, I could carry you back to the car through the rising waters."

Without any warning he swept her up in his arms and she gasped. "Don't drop me."

"Never." He kissed her until she was breathless, then put her gently back on her feet, where she leaned happily against him.

"Let's climb down and find some tide pools," Lorna suggested. "We could be surrounded by seals here and we'd never even know it with the fog."

Hand in hand they found a valley in the rocks where

the waves moved gently through a series of shallow pools. They sat down on a large, flat rock, their hands linked in the pocket of Jason's jacket, and waited patiently for something to happen. After several minutes a dark claw appeared from a crevice, plucked at a mossy plant, then disappeared. As they watched, not moving, several more crabs sidled cautiously into view and began feeding, their front claws moving rapidly between the rocks and their mouths.

"Shall we take some home for lunch?" Jason asked.

Lorna examined the inch-long crabs critically. "I hardly think Miriam would be grateful. And you'd never catch one anyway."

"Perhaps you're right." Jason glanced at his watch. "I suppose we'd better go back. Although I do like being out in the fog with you." He kissed her and she clung to him, pressing her thighs against his. His fingers stroked her hair, her cheeks, and she swayed a little, her foot slipping on the rocks.

He caught her elbows and pulled her against him so that she could feel quiet laughter moving his chest. "I think this spot is not as romantic as I thought," he told her. "I almost lost you to the waves."

Lorna shrugged. "It wasn't really that bad, but we probably should go before the waves do catch us."

Arm in arm they walked back to the car, encountering only one other couple on the beach. The drive back to Miriam's seemed very short, and once there Lorna went to the kitchen to help with lunch. She waited a little nervously to see if Miriam would say anything more about Jason's former girlfriends, but the topic seemed to have been exhausted, at least as far as Miriam was concerned.

After a lunch of bread and crab salad, Jason and Lorna loaded the dishwasher and then left for home. Lorna looked at the rocky coast out of the car window for a while, then turned resolutely to Jason.

"Somehow, in spite of the time we've spent together, I feel I don't know you very well," she told him.

"Well, I hope in time we'll get to know each other better." He took her hand, folding her fingers inside his own. "Would you like to spend midterm week with me in Vermont? I really want to get back there for a while, and I'd like to take you with me."

"I'd like that too," Lorna said. Perhaps he cared for her more than she thought. "I'll have to check my calendar to be sure, but I shouldn't have anything scheduled for that week. Once Coleman Grant leaves, I think I'm free."

"Fine." He squeezed her fingers, then returned his own to the steering wheel. "That will give us lots of time to get better acquainted."

When Lorna got home she called Beth right away. "He's invited me to Vermont week after next."

"I'm so glad. He must be serious about you then."

"I don't know." Suddenly she was less elated. "We haven't talked about the future. Sometimes I think I hardly know him."

"Are you in love with him?"

"Maybe. Yes." She bit her thumbnail. "I don't really know. But I care more for him than he does for me, I'm sure."

"Have you told him how you feel?"

"No. I guess I'm afraid of what he'd say." Lorna hung up soon after that and started a load of laundry, examining her clothes with disfavor. She'd have to look over her wardrobe and see what was suitable for a romantic trip to Vermont. Probably nothing. Most of her clothes were boring and utilitarian, especially the casual ones. Once she had disposed of Coleman Grant, she'd treat herself to a shopping spree.

Jason came over for dinner the next night, and she went to his cottage on the following evening. Each night his tenderness and sensitivity brought her such increasing delight that she marveled at how much had been missing from her life. She had never really believed it was possible for her to feel such a heady combination of love and desire. However or whenever the affair ended, she knew this was a time she would never regret.

With some effort she was able to concentrate on her work during the day. Coleman Grant was due to arrive Wednesday night for his lecture on Thursday, so Lorna was forced to pick him up at the airport instead of spending the evening with Jason. Grant's waspish criticisms of the local airport, Lorna's car, and her driving strained her determined good cheer, and she was relieved to abandon him at the motel. From that point on he'd be in the hands of the English department.

Once back at her house she decided against calling Jason. For one thing, she was in a rather irritable mood, and for another, she was a little afraid he might grow tired of her. She'd leave him alone for a night or two before they left for Vermont.

CHAPTER EIGHT

"What should I buy for a romantic week in Vermont?" she asked Fran over lunch on Friday, and Fran pursed her lips.

"Jeans, checked shirts, and mosquito repellent. I don't really know, and I'm almost too jealous to help you. I can guess who you're going with. Just find out what he likes women to wear, and take that, I guess."

Good advice, Lorna decided, and called Jason once she was back at her desk.

"Why the long silence?" he asked.

Lorna laughed. "In the first place, it's only been two days. In the second place, your phone has a dial on it as well as a receiver."

"All true. But when I pursue you, you seem to back away."

"Maybe I wouldn't do that anymore," she said softly. "Anyway, what clothes should I bring?"

"There'll just be you and me. I've given the caretakers the week off, so you won't need to wear anything at all. Just bring a toothbrush and some sturdy shoes."

"That's a charming picture." Lorna decided that on Friday afternoon she would go shopping even if she didn't know what she was looking for. Surely she could find something casual yet alluring if she really put her mind to it.

Friday evening she spread her new purchases out on the bed. The new jeans and pinstriped shirt were appropriate. She was less sure about a pair of skimpy magenta shorts and a white organdy blouse printed with magenta flowers. The outfit might be too flashy. With a shrug she tossed it in her suitcase along with several new sets of exotic underwear in various pastel shades. She added a frilly white camisole, which the saleswoman assured her looked very fetching with jeans or shorts. A few more pairs of jeans, several T-shirts, and some shoes, and she'd be packed. Jason was picking her up shortly after six the next morning, so there'd be little time then to get ready.

She eyed the neatly packed suitcase with a scowl. There still was not much inside it to inspire a man to passion. Suddenly apprehensive, she looked in the mirror, automatically smoothing her hair. This week would test their relationship, but perhaps it would also test her. Jason would be on his own turf, and he'd be watching to see how well she fit in. Her clothes probably would be the least of his interests, however. She took the suitcase downstairs and left it by the door, then went to bed.

She was ready when Jason arrived, and they set off immediately for the airport. "I think I've got a poem brewing," Jason said as he drove. "I can't wait to get home so I can sit down and work on it." He touched her cheek lightly. "I probably won't be very good company today."

"I'll buy a book in the airport," Lorna said.

Once on the plane, Jason became quite withdrawn, emerging from his reverie only when the flight attendant slid a plastic lunch tray onto his table.

"I've chartered a plane to take us from New York to St. Johnsbury," he told Lorna. "Connections are so mis-

137

erable, it's hardly worth struggling with the scheduled airlines. And today I'm particularly glad, since I'm so eager to get to work."

It appeared that the week in Vermont might not be quite what she had envisioned. If Jason was going to be locked up in an attic somewhere creating poetry, she'd have to keep out of his way. Seeing his eyes focus on some distant clouds, Lorna picked up her book again. This trip might be a true test of her self-reliance.

Several hours later she sighed happily as she and Jason walked across the airfield from the small charter plane that had brought them to Vermont.

"You didn't like that flight much, did you?" Jason smiled and Lorna managed an answering grin.

"It was a little bumpy, and the plane was so *small.*"

Jason stopped at a bright red and white Jeep. "The caretakers left this here for me a few days ago," he told Lorna as he loaded their bags in the back. "It's not always necessary at this time of year, I guess, but I prefer to use the Jeep on my roads, especially for fording the creek."

Lorna swallowed. "Is your house nearby?"

"It's south of here, near Peacham. I keep my roads very rough to discourage sightseers and the occasional autograph hunter, but of course what keeps others out also keeps me in, sometimes for weeks on end when the creek is high or the roads are slick with mud."

It was a stiff, bouncing journey in the high seats of the Jeep, even before they arrived at a narrow dirt road lined with sugar maples. Gentle green hills rolled off to the horizon, occasionally dotted with red barns or white clapboard houses. The ride grew rougher, the Jeep lurching over every hole and stone, and Lorna held tightly onto her seat.

"Is this part of Vermont uninhabited?" she asked finally. "I haven't seen a single person."

"There are farmhouses scattered around, but many of the owners work in town during the week now. It's back-breaking work to keep a Vermont farm solvent these days, and fewer and fewer people are inclined to try. It's always a surprise to see a neighbor here.

"This is the beginning of my road," Jason said about fifteen minutes later, stopping the Jeep to unlock a high padlocked gate that blocked a deeply rutted, rocky road. "There's an old saying," he said as Lorna gasped and they rocked over a series of small boulders. "In Vermont we have nine months of winter and three months of damn poor sledding. This is the poor sledding. In the winter, snow fills in the potholes and ruts and at times it's an easier drive than it is now. Except when the road drifts over."

Lorna was marveling at how dusty she had gotten in the last hour, when the Jeep made a sharp turn to the left and she had her first view of the house. Set on the side of a gentle forested hill, it was barely visible through the pine and maple trees. A hexagonal window on the second floor gleamed black in the fading light, and she kept her gaze fixed on that as the Jeep plunged down a steep bank into a rocky creek bed and climbed jerkily back up the other side.

"It's just as beautiful as I had imagined," she said a few minutes later, standing in front of the massive oak double doors.

"Come in." Jason unlocked the door, then with a sudden smile picked her up and carried her inside. "Welcome to Vermont," he murmured, kissing her soundly before setting her on her feet on the honey-colored wood floor.

"I'll put the Jeep away after dinner." He picked up

their suitcases and closed the front door firmly behind him.

It was terribly quiet, Lorna realized, as she followed him up the carpeted stairs. One bird was singing, and she could hear the faint sounds of some chirping insects. She and Jason might have been the only people left in the world.

"Why don't you wander around and get the feel of the place? I'll see what Mrs. Henshaw left us for dinner and pour us some wine." Jason deposited their suitcases inside a doorway at the end of the hall. "I assume you'll share my room." He looked at her and she nodded with a wide smile.

"Good." He went silently back down the stairs and Lorna was alone.

Jason's bedroom was rather spartan, she saw without much surprise. A tall cherrywood dresser, an ample bed with a brightly striped bedspread, and oyster-colored carpeting and curtains were the main items of furniture. There was a rather gloomy seascape over the bed—an icy ocean breaking on a gray beach dotted with white spume, and a threatening sky overhead. It wasn't like Miriam's work at all—more raw, almost frantic. She shivered and walked across the soft carpet to the connecting bathroom.

Pausing briefly at the peach-colored oversized tub, Lorna put her purse on the marble counter and combed her hair carefully, then freshened her lipstick. The wallpaper, striped in broad bands of taupe and peach, cast a flattering glow over her skin that made her smile with pleasure.

On her way back downstairs she stopped to look briefly into three other rooms along the corridor. One, apparently Jason's study, was piled high with books and loose papers, the walls lined with overflowing bookshelves. The next room seemed to be for guests, with pale blue twin beds, a dresser, and two small barrel chairs set by the window.

The last room was unfurnished except for a clear blue carpet and a painting that hung on one wall. It was the portrait of a young woman with gleaming black hair, her pale face covered with a network of fine lines as if it were cracked porcelain. Her rather sensuous mouth dropped with despair, and a tear glistened on one shattered cheek. Lorna crossed her arms over her chest as she stood in front of the picture. No wonder Jason hadn't put anything in this room. Who could stand to sleep or work in here under the tragic brown eyes of this tortured face?

She turned right at the bottom of the stairs and was greeted by a crackling fire in an enormous flagstone fireplace. Here the polished floor was covered with two large Chinese rugs, blue geometric patterns against cream-colored backgrounds. A long, angular blue sofa faced the fire, and in one corner a small group of upholstered chairs surrounded a bleached teak coffee table. The room was softly lit by lights hidden above the beams of the arching ceiling that rose up past the second floor to the roof of the house.

Lorna walked across to the dining room, where Jason was setting down a covered dish. The mahogany table was centered on a cinnabar rug with a black and cream border. Black-seated Chippendale chairs surrounded it, and several more stood to the side against one tobacco-colored wall.

"It's not quite chilly enough for a fire in the living room, but I couldn't resist," he told her, deftly opening a bottle of wine. "By the time we finish dinner we may be able to appreciate it."

"It's beautiful," Lorna said, sitting down at one end of the table, her back to an enormous window. Facing her was another painting, this one an autumn forest scene that picked up the colors of the rug and walls. Lorna knew very little about painting, but she was beginning to recognize the heavy brush strokes, muted colors, and the quality of despair she could see in this picture.

"Who is the artist?" she asked.

Jason didn't reply for a moment, and she looked at him quickly. His drawn face and rather distant look made her apprehensive, and she wished for a way to retract the question.

"I suppose this is as good a time as any to talk about this," he said slowly, and Lorna took a sip of her wine, her eyes focused on the smoky crystal goblet. "The pictures were painted by my ex-wife, Rachael. That was a self-portrait upstairs." He looked at Lorna for an instant and she nodded.

"She was a brilliant painter, and when we met I thought of myself as a talented young writer, ready to produce the great American novel. I was rebelling against my father, I guess, a very staid corporation lawyer. Anyway, I refused to go to college, much less law school. Rachael and I were married when I was eighteen." He shook his head and picked up his fork, then put it down again.

"It was a very tumultuous relationship—we were very young and very sure we had all the answers. It didn't take long for me to discover that Rachael was having affairs with many of my friends and with other men I didn't know. She was enraged that I expected her to be faithful to me, said that sexual freedom was essential to her creativity. I was shattered, completely disillusioned in what I had thought was a great love. And so I left her after weeks of fierce arguments. And to make sure I would never have such a painful experience again, I gave up writing, abandoned all my friends, went back to school, and followed in my father's footsteps.

"A few years later I saw these paintings in a gallery. I bought them with some idea of helping Rachael, I guess. They were priced very low, and I gathered she wasn't selling much. I grew to like them, although some people find them depressing. By now I'm used to having them around."

"Anyway, I never fell in love again, never remarried."

Lorna met his eyes. "It must have been terrible to go through something like that when you were so young."

"I'm not sure it would be any easier now." He shrugged as if to dismiss her sympathy. "I suppose I was very naive. Imagine getting married first and then discovering we disagreed about something as fundamental as sexual fidelity."

"There never are any guarantees." Lorna turned sideways to face him fully, wanting very much to preserve the intimacy of the moment. "I thought my husband and I agreed about most things, but everything changed somehow when I started working. I guess I didn't need him as much, or at least I felt more confident, so he found someone else who was more dependent and wanted to be taken care of at any price. And at that point I guess I had already known the marriage was over, although it was still hard to accept." She dropped her eyes, embarrassed to hear a quiver in her voice.

"And a year later it still hurts?" His voice was gentle.

"The memory hurts, I guess," she said softly. "It's not that I would change anything now."

"Neither would I." His hand covered hers warmly where it lay on the table, and she turned to him quickly, resting her other hand on his knee. "Come with me in front of the fire," he said in a low voice, standing and pulling her to her feet.

She was hopelessly in love with him, she thought later, lying with him naked and content in front of the fire. And he might not ever be ready to fall in love again. He had protected himself all these years since his divorce, buried himself in his work, and kept his feelings locked inside. But of course there had always been women. She had no reason to think that her position was any different from other women he had known.

"Let's go to bed," she said suddenly, shivering a little despite the heat of the fire. "I'll do the dishes tomorrow."

"In the morning I'll show you the pond," he murmured after he turned the bedroom light out. "And the wild raspberry bushes." His breathing deepened and she knew he was asleep. Lorna lay awake for nearly an hour, staring at the ceiling as the moon shone coldly through the window.

CHAPTER NINE

She awoke in the morning to a mad chorus of birdsong, and realized that Jason was already up. Feeling a little abandoned, she walked to the window, hugging herself against the cool breeze that played across her skin. Looking through the branches of the tall pine tree that sheltered the side of the house, she could see the gentle rise of a green hill with a narrow dirt track running around its side. There was not a car or a person to be seen. She stood there for a few minutes, rubbing her arms to keep warm, then walked quickly to the shower.

She went downstairs dressed in her new jeans and camisole to find a note next to a glass of freshly squeezed orange juice. "Upstairs writing," it read. "Dishes washed. Coffee and cereal in the kitchen. Down by ten."

She glanced at her watch and saw that it was eight thirty. There wouldn't be a morning newspaper, obviously, but maybe she could find a book to read with breakfast. She always read when she ate alone. After a fruitless search downstairs, she went upstairs, running her hand slowly along the smooth oak bannister. The hexagonal window she had seen from the Jeep was at the end of the hall, she saw, where it framed a stand of shimmering birch trees. The study door was open only a crack, and Jason was obviously behind it, hard at work. And every book in the house was in there with him. She didn't want to disturb him. Disappointed, she got a sweater out of her suitcase and went back downstairs. She might as well postpone breakfast and go for a walk. She almost wished he had left the dishes. It would have given her something to do.

Drinking half her orange juice, she went out the kitchen door, carefully leaving it unlocked behind her. There was a vegetable garden and a flower garden, and farther away a small cottage that probably housed the Henshaws. She followed a dirt track past the cottage and downhill to a creek, where she perched on a convenient boulder. The sun was heating the air, and she took off her sweater, tilting her head back for a moment to warm her face. The air smelled clean and damp, and she inhaled deeply.

She started nervously as Jason's hand fell on her shoulder. "Here you are! I thought I'd lost you."

"Is it ten?"

"Not quite. Let's put together a picnic and we can take the Jeep to the pond. It should be warm enough to swim today."

"I didn't think to bring a suit." After all of her agonizing over what clothes to bring, she had actually forgotten something.

He laughed loudly. "This isn't the community swimming pool. There's no one around for miles, so a swim suit would be superfluous." As she hesitated, he shook his head. "There won't be anyone there but me, and in case you've forgotten, I'm quite intimately acquainted with your body. Although there's always more to learn," he added, pulling her close with one arm around her waist, his hand resting lightly on her hip.

She flushed a little. "I guess I've never been so far

away from civilization. I can't help thinking that as soon as I take off my clothes two boy scout troops and a ladies' auxiliary will appear among the trees."

He shrugged. "It would be a positive educational experience for them, I'm sure. Let's just go and play it by ear. I can probably loan you a pair of trunks, if that would help."

They sliced some ham and tomatoes and Jason discovered a bowl of potato salad in the refrigerator. "Mrs. Henshaw usually leaves me plenty to eat for the first few days," he said as he packed everything into a straw basket. "It's just a matter of figuring out what menus she had in mind."

They bounced off in the Jeep toward the creek along the track and then along a faint path through a meadow. "Here we are," Jason announced as the Jeep gave one final lurch over a protruding tree root, and Lorna gladly stepped out into the shade of an oak tree while Jason spread a thick quilt over a nearby bed of pine needles. The air was very still and warm, and she wished she had worn her shorts.

Jason stretched out on his back, his hands clasped behind his head. "It's good to be back here, and I'm glad you're here with me," he said.

Lorna leaned down to kiss him, her lips soft on his sun-warmed mouth. She loved the faint scent of his skin when it was not obscured by aftershave lotion or soap. It smelled very clean and masculine. Filled with tenderness, she kissed his face in scores of different places, one hand resting over his heart as her lips sought out the most sensitive areas around his eyes and mouth.

He drew a deep breath, his chest rising under her hand, and she lifted her head to look at him. His khaki pants were faded and worn, especially around the knees, and his blue T-shirt had a tiny tear in one shoulder seam.

He seemed so familiar, so much a part of her life, that it was hard to remember that there were still times when he was almost like a stranger. There was so much she had yet to learn about him.

He lifted one hand to her hair and raised a strand to let it fall gradually back in place. "Your hair is so pale, it shimmers in the light," he said. "It's like filaments of crystal."

She put her hand to his head, which was surprisingly hot in the few places where the sun shone down through the branches, and ran her fingers through the dark curls. She stroked the traces of gray at his temples, then leaned down to kiss him again, her tongue delicately tracing the inner line of his lips. She pulled his T-shirt free and ran her hand flat along his chest, up over his ribs, and then down across his stomach. The arm supporting her weight grew tired and she sat up, her other hand still resting lightly under his ribs.

His eyes were very dark, hardly even blue, and there was a faint smile on his lips as he reached up to unfasten the tiny pearl buttons on her camisole. A warm breeze caressed her as she slipped out of the lacy top, and she paused for a second in surprise. She had never been naked out of doors, she realized, and automatically glanced around at the surrounding trees.

"There's no one here but you and me," Jason said. "I promise."

She leaned down and breathed lightly into his ear. "That's easy for you to say when you have all your clothes on."

He sat up and pulled off his T-shirt in one easy motion, and she put her arms around him to bring his chest against her breasts. His skin was warm, and she pulled away a little to taste the hollow at the base of his neck. Her hand fumbled at the snap of his slacks as she nibbled gently at the nerve-rich spot above his collarbone, and she felt enormously elated when he moaned her name. He wanted her, no one else, she thought as he carefully unzipped her jeans. And she couldn't imagine being without him, or being any other place but where she was at that moment. Her hips moved with sudden urgency and she reached out to him, caressing him intimately as she drew him to her.

"I'll do whatever you want, whatever makes you happy," he told her, his breath warm against her shoulder.

"Love me," she whispered, expressing for the first time her growing knowledge of what she needed from him.

"Yes, I'll love you," he answered, kissing her cheeks, then her eyelids as she arched up against him. "I'll never stop loving you."

She forgot where they were, forgot everything but Jason, who had said he would love her forever. He was more tender and yet more urgent than he had ever been, and his body told her that he, too, was vulnerable, that he needed her. She caressed and soothed him with her hands, aching to express the depth of her own love, wanting somehow to show him that he could rely on her. When the sensations of their bodies finally overtook her, she cried out that she loved him, and tears pricked her eyes for an instant as he kissed her fiercely.

Afterward they lay together a long time without speaking, their bodies entwined on the quilt. Lorna looked up at the pine branches, caressing Jason's head where it rested against her shoulder. He'd never said he loved her except in the throes of desire, she reminded herself, and she was hardly in a position to ask for more. She was the one who had said she didn't want to become too deeply involved. She'd tried until recently to keep some distance between them, to prevent herself from wanting him at the expense of her own independence. By now she felt absolutely certain that there was more between them than physical attraction, more than the obvious chemistry. It was frightening, but it was exhilarating too. She wouldn't resist her growing feelings for him if he gave her further signs that he, too, was falling in love. And somehow just then it was hard to believe that he felt any different from the way she did.

She sighed, stretching languidly on the quilt. She reveled in her nakedness in the open air. The piny smell of the trees, the songs of the birds, and the faint water sounds of the pond combined with the warm breezes on her skin to make her feel freer and less inhibited than she'd ever been.

Jason leaned over and kissed her lightly. "Shall we have a swim?"

"Sure." She stood up gracefully and walked carefully to the edge of the water, pine needles and a few pebbles pricking the soles of her feet.

"It's cold!" she announced after testing the water with one foot. "I don't think I can go in."

"Nonsense." Jason scooped her up in his arms and began walking out into the water. "The secret is to get it over with." He tossed her unceremoniously into the pond and she surfaced gasping, shaking her hair out of her eyes.

"Bully!" she laughed, splashing water toward his face. "Why don't you pick on someone your own size?"

He raised his hands, shaking the water out of his hair. "There's no one here but you."

She swam quickly to the other side of the pond, then floated back easily, watching a few fluffy clouds move over the sun. Jason swam past her and left the water.

"Luncheon is served," he called a few moments later, and she kicked out toward shore.

After lunch they lay quietly in each other's arms, and Jason seemed to sleep for a few minutes. Lorna watched him contentedly, admiring his faintly lined forehead, his narrow, straight nose, and his slightly parted lips. Cautiously she stroked a lock of hair off his forehead, then ran one finger lightly around the curve of his ear. Smiling to herself, she watched a pair of birds fly back and forth among the branches over her head until Jason's sudden movement told her he was awake.

"Let's walk around a little," he suggested.

Lorna looked down at her white skin.

"Like this? Let me get dressed first."

They spent most of the afternoon walking around the pond, and returned to the Jeep tired and stained with raspberry juice. Lorna climbed into her seat and leaned back, grateful for the relative softness of the cushion. Jason got in, but did not start the car.

"You know," he said suddenly, and she turned to him. "It seems so right having you here. It's like suddenly finding the part that's been missing from my life. I've been thinking." He paused and she looked at him, her heart seeming to beat high in her throat. "I think I want to marry you," he said abruptly, and her eyes widened.

"I'm in love with you," she answered slowly, "and I think I have been for a long time. But you've never said you loved me until today."

"For a man who calls himself a poet, I'm not doing a very good job of this, am I?" He smiled wryly and she reached for his hand. "I love you very much. I think I fell in love with you when I first saw you in your office. I could imagine you sleeping in my arms, your head on my shoulder. And then when I first went to your house, it seemed so welcoming to me, a place I could easily live in myself. We fit together."

She leaned over to kiss him, her hand stroking his

cheek as her lips caressed his. "I like talking with you, cooking dinner with you, making love with you," he went on, looking intently into her eyes. "And you know, you've never said you loved me until today either."

She embraced him quickly, then moved as close to him as she could, her hand resting on his thigh. "I think I'd like to marry you," she told him, "but I want to be certain. I know I love you, but we haven't known each other very long." It was hard to be cautious now, but they both had learned the consequences of hasty marriages. "Let's just take our time, and be very, very sure we know it's right for both of us."

"I think that's probably a good idea. I just wanted you to know my intentions." He kissed her very tenderly. "Don't imagine for a minute that I invited you here light-heartedly, or that I don't take this very seriously. I know you were afraid of me, and I never would have pursued you if I hadn't believed things could be this good between us."

She moved a little closer to him and her knee bumped the gearshift. "I can't even kiss you properly in this Jeep," she complained, and he grinned.

"Naturally, I picked the most romantic spot for my proposal. I just wanted to make sure there was no question of my having to kneel."

Lorna laughed, bubbling over with happiness. "Let's go back to the house and celebrate," she said, and he turned the key in the ignition.

"Wait," Lorna said suddenly, and got out to carefully pick a ladybug off the windshield and toss it toward the edge of the road. "I don't want anything to be unhappy today," she told Jason, laying her hand on his thigh.

As they bounced along the track she beamed at the trees, the birds, even the clouds on the horizon. Everything in the world was absolutely perfect. She was sitting next to the man she loved, the most wonderful man she had ever met, and he was in love with her. They were alone together in a beautiful spot, and they had the rest of the week to enjoy each other. She felt supremely secure, knowing that nothing could interfere with her happiness.

"Why didn't you ever marry again?" she asked Jason as they drank champagne at the kitchen table, and he smiled.

"Maybe I wasn't ready, or maybe it's because I hadn't met you yet." He seemed to consider her for a moment. "You have a lot of qualities I admire. You're capable and independent, but you're still soft and loving. And I can be myself with you—I don't have to act like a lawyer or a poet or anyone but me, even if I'm a little silly at times." He smiled and she put her glass down to take his hands. "I just feel very good when I'm with you," he said, pulling her on to his lap.

"You make me very happy," Lorna whispered, and nestled against him. It would take years and volumes of words to fully express how she felt.

"We have lots of plans to make," Jason told her over dinner. "I'll be moving back here in September, and I'd hate for us to be apart for any length of time."

Lorna's fingers were suddenly ice cold. "You mean, if we got married, we'd live here?"

"Of course." Jason gestured with his wineglass toward the windows. "You'll see how wonderful it can be, just the two of us. In the winter it's astonishingly beautiful. All the trees are heavy with snow, and the ground is completely white and trackless. At sunrise and sunset the snow turns delicate shades of blue and pink. And in the spring there are wildflowers everywhere. The autumn is beyond my powers of description, I think. I've been trying to write a poem about the colors for a year—cinnamon, tangerine, magenta."

Lorna nodded. "It's lovely here, I know, and very comfortable. I just hadn't thought about quitting my job. And everything," she finished lamely, looking unhappily at her plate.

"Are you saying no?"

"No, I'm not." Lorna reached out to him impulsively, shaken at the idea of losing him.

"You'll see how happy we can be." He looked at her seriously for a moment, then smiled. "I'm looking forward to keeping you warm through the long winter nights."

The next morning Lorna again found Jason gone when she got up. At least she had had the foresight to borrow a few books from his study before they had gone to bed. Once they were married, she'd have to make sure she was well supplied with reading material. What would she do all day? Mr. and Mrs. Henshaw took care of everything, it seemed, and Jason would hardly want to lose them. Even if Lorna took over some of the household chores, there wouldn't be enough to keep her busy. And it was hard to imagine finding a satisfying job in this rural part of Vermont.

"We can start a family," Jason said when she told him her fears. "That will give you plenty to do, and it's something I've wanted for a long time. This is a great place for children to grow up—they'd have so much more freedom than most children and they'd learn so much about nature."

"Children need playmates, too, and schools," Lorna said doubtfully. "And I don't think it's a good idea to start a family just because I'm bored."

Jason planted a kiss on her nose. "Plenty of rural Vermonters have kids. You'll see, it will all work out."

"I'm trying to believe that. I guess I need more time to think." Lorna smiled weakly.

"Well, I've found this a great place to think things through." He hesitated. "Would you mind very much if I went back upstairs and did a little more work? You've inspired me to new heights, and I don't want to stop when things are going so well."

She shook her head and he kissed her before he ran up the stairs. Her book was waiting on the back porch, but perhaps she should take a walk. Armed with a book about the birds of North America, she walked back down the dirt track toward the gate, painstakingly looking up every bird she saw.

"I think I found a hairy woodpecker, a horned lark, and a lot of sparrows," she told Jason that evening, and he raised his eyebrows.

"I didn't know you were a birdwatcher."

"I thought I'd become one," she explained, "if I'm going to live out here in the country."

The next day she cooked a chicken in the morning and made Chinese chicken salad for dinner. In the afternoon she made bread, filling the house with the warm yeasty aroma, then weeded the kitchen garden when the sun was moving lower in the sky. She picked a bouquet of bright pink phlox, cosmos, and purple dahlias, and arranged them in a flared Italian vase. Jason appeared for the first time just before dinner, looking tired and rumpled.

"I'm working on a love poem," he told her, smiling softly, "and it's really going well. I can hardly wait to finish it."

"Are you going back to work after dinner?" she asked, and he frowned.

"No, I want to spend some time with you. Have you been lonely?" At her nod, he went on. "Maybe I've been insensitive, leaving you by yourself so much. I feel as if you belong here, but you probably still feel like a neglected guest. Maybe you'd like to take the Jeep into the village tomorrow and look around. There's quite a nice community of summer people—and a good little library."

Lorna nodded. "I could pick up some groceries, too, and do some more cooking. It's fun to have the free time, but . . ."

"But what?" He looked over at her, and she twisted her fork between her fingers.

"I guess I'm not used to having so much free time. It will take me a while to get used to it."

The next day, as Jason had suggested, she took the long drive into the village, flushed with triumph at having negotiated the crossing of the creek. There was a country store, a men's club, a small museum, and a church. The library wouldn't be open for another hour, and the museum would not open at all that day. She stocked up on groceries, carefully storing the perishables in the ice chest she had brought in the Jeep. The man in the store, probably the owner, was polite but unresponsive to Lorna's attempts at conversation. Jason had told her that Vermonters could be somewhat clannish, treating even long-standing residents as outsiders if they were "from away."

The librarian was much friendlier, and when Lorna confided her plans the woman piled her arms with books of local history.

"I've never lived in the country before," Lorna said. "It seems rather quiet."

The librarian smiled. "I know. I used to be a summer person here. My husband fished all day and I puttered around wondering what to do with myself. But when you live here year round, you get so many projects under way that there's never enough time."

"But you have your job," Lorna reminded her.

"That's true. Although winter hours are much shorter. I don't get much business then."

Seeing another patron waiting for attention, Lorna left with a promise to return her books at the end of the week. It felt wonderful to have had a conversation with someone other than Jason. She strolled up to the white church, admiring its tall, tapering spire. It had won an architecture award, Jason had told her. It was easy to imagine how it would appear on a cold winter day, surrounded by bare branches and white snow, the spire reaching into the leaden clouds. Glancing at her watch, she decided to start back. Jason might come down for lunch today.

The ride home was uneventful until she encountered three cows on the dirt road, all of whom seemed disinclined to move no matter how often she tooted the Jeep's horn. Made brave by hunger, she finally left the car and confronted the nearest cow, a rather unattractive brown and white splotched specimen. Close up, the cow seemed unusually large, more formidable than a horse.

"Shoo!" Lorna said unconvincingly, making pushing motions with her hands, and the cow shuffled its feet a little. They *were* all cows, she hoped as she backed carefully toward the Jeep. What if one turned out to be a bull? Safely back in her seat, she checked each one for udders, then, satisfied that she wouldn't be gored on the spot, she leaned on the Jeep's horn. At least she didn't have to worry about annoying the neighbors with her noise. Although it would have been nice to hope that someone would come and collect his stray cattle.

She didn't have the courage to leave the road and drive the Jeep through the trees and around the cows. She was afraid to try to force the cows to move. Would she have to sit in the Jeep all afternoon? Ready to cry from frustration, she started the engine and rolled the Jeep forward, stopping a few inches from the spotted cow, who obligingly shuffled four centimeters down the road. Lorna tapped the gas pedal again, and made another few inches of progress. Wonderful. At this rate she might be at the house by morning.

A brown cow approached, tossing her head nervously, and seemed to look Lorna straight in the eye before settling comfortably down in a shady hollow in the road. The other two cows ambled nearer, obviously ready to follow suit.

"That does it!" Lorna jumped out of the Jeep and selected a large rock, which she threw deliberately at the brown cow's rump before hurrying back into the Jeep. With a loud *moo,* the cow scrambled up and lurched off to gaze at Lorna mournfully from beneath a tree, and her two companions reluctantly followed suit. Somewhat shaken, Lorna started forward again. With any luck she had only the creek to face, and then she'd be at Jason's.

He was in the kitchen making a sandwich when she came in, and she kissed him warmly. The events of the morning seemed rather unexciting when she recounted them, but he listened attentively as he sliced a crumbly block of Cheddar cheese.

"I'm glad you're learning your way around," he said as she bit into her sandwich.

"I'm afraid I'll never be a country girl."

"By next year," he laughed, "you'll be raising goats and chickens."

Goats and chickens? Lorna eyed the garden speculatively after Jason had gone back upstairs. He had started a light chowder for dinner, and she was free to take a walk. After some thought she decided to go back to the pond. It was a long walk, but she wouldn't get lost, and if she got too warm on the way she could always take a swim once she had arrived.

It was hot and dusty along the track, and she wished she had thought of bringing something to drink. The pond water might not be potable, and then she would have the long, thirsty walk home. Out here there were no convenience stores. She would have to learn to plan ahead.

Reluctantly she turned back, having gone three-quarters of the way. She dragged her feet a little in the dust of the road, wishing there were a little more shade. Maybe she could plant some fast-growing trees after she and Jason were married. Her mouth was very dry, and her tongue seemed to be made of cotton. It was eerie to be the only person for a mile or more, she thought as she sat down under a tree.

Wiping her forehead with the back of her hand, she sighed. If only Jason had come with her instead of going back to work. She forced a bright smile as she heard the sound of an engine, and when the red Jeep appeared around a curve in the road, she stood up and waved vigorously.

"I decided to join you," Jason said, looking at her speculatively. "Have you already had your swim?"

"No, I got thirsty." She climbed into the Jeep, wincing as the back of her knees touched the hot seat.

"Have some lemonade." Jason handed her a large insulated pitcher and a cup. "Shall I drive you to the pond?"

The lemonade was tart and cold. In fact, she had never tasted better. She looked happily at Jason's profile, her mood suddenly lifted. The pond, once they reached it, was wonderfully refreshing, and after a leisurely swim Lorna felt clean and cool.

"Maybe I should rinse my clothes too," she told Jason, squeezing the water out of her hair as she balanced carefully on a small tuft of grass.

"Only if you're willing to ride home as you are," Jason said. "I've never let anyone sit in the Jeep in wet shorts. Even in your case, I'm unlikely to make an exception. In fact, I'm rather intrigued by the possibilities. An unclothed woman riding around in a Jeep is just bizarre enough to be very tempting."

Lorna turned away slightly, suddenly conscious of her nakedness. "I'll just wear them dusty then," she decided, stepping awkwardly into her pants.

Jason's hands were warm on her shoulders. "Are you happy here?" he asked, and she nodded, leaning back until her head tucked securely under his chin.

They had fallen into a schedule that seemed to suit Jason's work habits. He got up early and went into his study, where he stayed until early afternoon. In the mornings Lorna walked, worked in the garden, or read. She made lunch for them and Jason washed the dishes. After that they would take a walk together or drive the Jeep to the pond. Jason seemed to enjoy cooking dinner, and since he was clearly a better cook than Lorna, she decided not to protest.

"It relaxes me," he told her, deftly slicing a bunch of green onions. "And of course women find it very impressive."

Lorna studied her fingernails. "I guess sometime I'll have to hear about your lurid past," she said finally, struggling for a light tone.

He put the knife down carefully and ran a finger gently across her cheek to her lips. "There've been other women, I don't deny that. But I was never in love with any of them, not even for a few seconds, so don't waste your time worrying about them."

She smiled into his serious blue eyes. "All right."

He kissed her softly on the nose before turning back to

the dinner. "That was certainly easy. I hope we'll be able to solve all our problems so smoothly."

Of course they would have problems, Lorna reminded herself as she set the table with his black-rimmed porcelain plates. This romantic idyll couldn't last forever, and she was mature enough not to expect it to. There was no reason to find Jason's remark ominous, but she felt uneasy nevertheless.

She lay awake that night, listening to the low call of an owl as Jason slept peacefully beside her, one of his arms lying warmly across her waist. Carefully she put one hand over his, choking back a sudden rush of tears as he awakened briefly and snuggled up to her. Jason was caring and sensitive, a man she loved more than she would ever have thought possible, but she was beginning to worry that love might not be enough.

She was tired and gloomy the next morning, their last full day in Vermont, and took a long walk to improve her mood before Jason came down for lunch. It was a cloudy day, and somehow very quiet. The birds were silent, no wind moved through the trees, and her own steps along the dirt track made only the faintest of noises. Jason was probably the only other human being for twenty or thirty miles around. She stood there in the road, gazing at the horizon through a sudden veil of tears until she could hardly see at all.

Wiping away the tears with her fingers, she spun around and began walking quickly back to the house. This once, she would have to interrupt Jason while he was working. What she had to say couldn't wait; she could so easily lose her courage.

"I've been looking for you," he said as she opened the kitchen door. "I've finished the poem."

His satisfaction was so apparent, she resolved not to rob him of the enjoyment, and managed a small smile as he handed her several sheets of paper. "For Lorna," she read at the top of the first sheet, and felt the tears start again.

"I knew it might need a few revisions, but I didn't think it was bad enough to make you cry." He smiled tenderly, but she recognized the question in his eyes. Shaking her head miserably, she laid the papers unread on the kitchen table.

"I can't marry you, Jason," she said, turning away from the pain she saw etched on his face. "I love you, and I guess I'll always love you, but I can't live here like this, so cut off from everything."

"Is it only that? That you don't want to move out here?" he asked, and she turned back to look at him, suddenly hopeful. Perhaps Vermont meant less to him than she had thought. Maybe he'd say they could go somewhere else, anywhere else, as long as there were other people around, and things to do.

"If it's really that, and not something to do with me, then I don't think there's a problem," he said slowly, and she threw her arms around his neck. "The isolation takes time to get used to, that's all. But I'm sure you'll settle in. You're a very independent woman, after all."

"I'm not independent in that way," she told him, her ribs aching as she slowly pulled away to sit in a kitchen chair. "I enjoy being with friends, meeting new people. And I love my job. I could say I'd give it all up for you, but I know I'd be miserable and I'd make you miserable too."

He stood looking down at her, his hands in his pockets, and she couldn't bear to meet his eyes. "I need this solitude," he said quietly. "If there are people around, and other things to do, I don't write poetry. And that work is very important to me right now. I don't want to spend my life giving readings of my old poems and signing autographs in books I wrote years ago. I love it here. This is where I belong." As he gestured to include everything around them, Lorna sighed. There were no more tears now, just the cold realization that the fantasy was over.

"I wouldn't ask you to give up anything for me," she told him, "not your work or your home. It would poison everything between us. And by the same token, I don't want to give up everything for you."

She looked around the blue and white kitchen. After tomorrow she wouldn't see the hand-painted ceramic tiles again, or the spacious wooden cupboards where she had planned to put her china. "I think I'll go up to the bedroom for a while."

"Shall I make you a sandwich?"

She still couldn't meet his eyes. "I'm not very hungry," she said after a few seconds. "Maybe I'll skip lunch."

He turned to walk to the refrigerator, his steps leaden, and she slipped quietly out of her chair and ran upstairs, closing the bedroom door gently behind her. The tears she expected, even wanted, didn't come, and she leaned on the windowsill for a long time, reliving over and over the scene she had just left. Finally, knowing she had to face him eventually, she went back to the kitchen to find Jason polishing a plate with a checkered dishtowel.

"You never read the poem," he reminded her in a level voice, and she fought down a treacherous surge of emotion.

"I don't think I can just now. Maybe in a few days."

He nodded. "Would you like to take a walk?"

She opened the kitchen door and stepped out to the path, waiting for him to join her. When he took her hand she squeezed his tightly for an instant, then released her grip as they walked slowly toward the pond.

"I'm sorry," she said suddenly, after they had walked in silence for nearly an hour.

"I'm sorry too." His face was expressionless, offering neither understanding nor forgiveness.

"If I thought there was a chance I could make you happy, I'd be willing to try," Lorna whispered plaintively. "But I'd go crazy here."

They walked the rest of the way in a kind of sad, silent communion, and stopped at the shady spot where they had made love on their first visit to the pond. Jason gave a short, bitter laugh and turned away when Lorna sat down on the grass. She pulled her knees up, resting her head on her hands to hide her face.

"I still can't believe this is happening to us," she said, and he faced her immediately, his lips in a tight line.

"This is not something that's happening." He bit off the ends of every word and she flinched away from the anger in his voice. "This is something *you're* doing, with very little forethought, because you're afraid to take a chance. I thought you had more courage." He shrugged, as if to dismiss her from his life altogether.

"I don't have the courage to go through another divorce, that's true. And this would end in divorce. I've never had any desire to live a solitary life, to putter around by myself. I love my work. It's very important to me. What kind of work could I do here? Show people around the museum for one hour a week? Stand behind the counter in the country store?

"I'd be living just for you, waiting every day for you to come downstairs and talk to me. I wouldn't be myself anymore, can't you understand that?"

"I understand that you don't want to share my life. That's all I need to understand."

She watched his back with wide, shocked eyes as he walked up the track in the direction of the house. She'd be alone on the way back, obviously. With a shrug she took off her sandals and moved closer to the pond so she could wiggle her toes in the water. She wasn't going to run after Jason, nor did she want to look at his stiff back all the way home. If he was as insensitive as his last remarks had shown, she didn't want to be with him anyway. They could just stay away from each other until the ride to the airport.

The walk back from the pond seemed so long, she wondered at one point if she was lost, and once she was back in the house she lay on the bed in the room they had shared, staring at the ceiling until her watch told her it was nearly dinnertime.

Before she ate the salad she made, she carefully cleared the kitchen of any signs of her presence. Tossing a lettuce core into the garbage can, she caught a glimpse of crumpled papers and, suddenly suspicious, removed them carefully to smooth them out on the tile counter.

As she had guessed, Jason had thrown the love poem away. Surely at some later time he would regret that gesture. Careful not to read the handwritten words, Lorna folded the papers and put them deep into the pocket of her slacks before she took her salad out the back door. There was a small grassy area near the Henshaws' cottage, and since they were away she felt free to eat her dinner there. It would be pleasant and private—not that anyone other than Jason was likely to see her even if she chose to eat in the middle of the road.

She picked at her salad, finally leaving it half eaten on the grass while she strolled around the garden to remove any weeds. Once the sun had almost set and the danger of meeting Jason in the kitchen was gone, she picked up her salad bowl and carried it through the back door. It slipped from her fingers and cracked on the floor as she saw Jason reading a book at the kitchen table.

"I'll help you," he said as she knelt to pick up the scattered salad and pieces of the bowl, but she shook her head. "You'll cut yourself," he added sharply, holding out his hand to take the shards she had collected. "Why don't you concentrate on mopping up the dressing." Wordlessly she did as he suggested, jerking away quickly when his arm brushed hers.

"I'll sleep in the guest bedroom tonight," she said suddenly, as if the brief touch of his forearm against her skin had reminded her of the passionate nights they'd spent together. He gave no indication that he had heard, but carefully disposed of the last traces of her accident.

She stood up as he washed his hands and threw the wet paper towel in the garbage, and she looked away feeling guilty about the poem she had tucked away in her pocket. Jason looked at her for a moment, then pulled her abruptly to his chest, his fingers digging almost painfully into her soft upper arms.

"Maybe I can change your mind," he murmured, his voice deeper than ever, and she twisted her head away as his lips sought hers. One of his hands moved to her buttocks, pressing her lower back firmly against him as his other hand roamed freely over her breasts.

"At least you still feel something for me," he said as her breathing quickened, and she wrenched desperately away.

"Don't do this to me, Jason," she said brokenly, looking directly into his darkened eyes. "I can't bear it."

He released her without warning and lifted one shoulder slightly, a cynical smile twisting his lips. "All right. I'll go move your things."

"Thank you." She sank down on a chair, her knees trembling so violently she felt as if she would never be able to stand up.

"I won't bother you again." He looked at her for a moment, then turned to go upstairs.

CHAPTER TEN

They ate breakfast like polite strangers who unexpectedly find themselves forced to share a table until Jason said, "I guess I was ready to make the same mistake twice, even after all these years."

"What mistake was that?" Lorna asked.

"Deciding to get married without discussing all the important issues. We both know that true love doesn't solve every problem."

"Well, we didn't get married; we just talked about it. Anyway," she went on, "this was really my fault. I wanted to live with you, and for a while I thought I could."

"I could have saved us both a lot of pain by asking a few questions first," Jason insisted.

"I think we have to share the responsibility." Lorna felt her throat tighten. "When we get back to Crowley . . ."

"Yes?" He looked at her.

"Will we still see each other?"

Jason rubbed his hand across his forehead. "I don't know," he said finally. "I hate to say good-bye, but maybe it's best. At least let's not see each other for a while. Let's let things settle down."

"Okay."

Lorna washed the dishes, blinking back tears, while Jason loaded the Jeep. Then she climbed carefully into the passenger seat, her library books tucked under one arm.

"I hope we have time for a quick stop at the library. I forgot to take these books back."

Jason started the Jeep, facing straight ahead. "We have plenty of time if you'd like to stop off there."

They didn't speak again until the Jeep was outside the library. "I'll just be a minute," Lorna promised, and hurried into the small building. The librarian accepted the books with a warm smile.

"I'll look forward to getting to know you better in the fall," she said as Lorna turned to leave, and Lorna hesitated, brushing her hair back while she chose her words.

"It doesn't look as if I'll be moving here after all," she said quietly, not turning around. "I'm going back to California for good."

"Oh, dear. I hope I haven't put my foot in my mouth." The older woman approached to put her hand lightly on Lorna's arm. "I'm sure everything will work out for the best."

Lorna nodded, not trusting herself to speak. With a tiny smile she went back to the Jeep and took her seat, never looking at Jason. He started the car without a word and they drove in silence all the way to the airport. It was not as if they had talked a great deal on the trip up. But there had been no constraint between them. Jason's hand had rested on her knee from time to time, and she had been busy taking in all the details that she could see from the Jeep. Everything had seemed strange and new to her, and rather exciting. Now the gently rolling green landscape seemed foreign and hostile. She couldn't wait to leave, to go back to the dry, golden summer hills she was accustomed to.

The plane ride seemed interminable, although Lorna managed to sleep a few hours during the second flight. Jason's face was worn, his eyes shadowed and tired, she noticed as she reached across him for her lunch tray. Her own appearance was probably not much better. She had been awake most of the night, casting desperately for a way to resolve things between them and salvage their relationship. Once they were back in California it would be too easy to avoid each other. Everything would truly be over then.

No solution had come to her in the night, and none came to her that day. As Jason's rental car pulled into her driveway she bit her lip, suddenly afraid that she might disrupt the delicately maintained balance between them by being unable to say good-bye. She shifted in her seat as Jason turned off the ignition, looking at him directly for the first time that day.

"I guess this is the end," she said softly, and he nodded.

"It could be worse," he added, with one of the cynical smiles she was coming to dread. "At least you don't have to worry about what to do with an engagement ring."

"That certainly makes me feel better." She opened the door of the car and stepped out, wondering if he was going to get out with her. "I'll get my own bag," she said finally, seeing that he didn't move.

She pulled it awkwardly off the backseat as Jason suddenly jumped out of the car to take it from her.

"This is ridiculous," he said harshly, carrying the bag to her doorstep and putting it down. "There's no reason for us to part on bad terms. Things just didn't work out, that's all."

She nodded and followed him to her door, tears welling in her eyes for the first time. She found her keys and unlocked the door clumsily, her shaking hands making it hard to fit the key into the lock.

"Let's say good-bye in a nice way," Jason said as she turned to him, and she stiffened as he put his hands on her arms. "Don't be afraid," he whispered as he pulled her close to him, and she shook her head wordlessly, her body trembling.

"Take care of yourself." He pushed her away suddenly and walked to his car as she watched, tears spilling down her cheeks.

She turned abruptly and picked up her bag, unwilling to stand and watch him drive away. Once behind the door she dropped the bag heavily on the floor and sank onto the sofa cushions as if she were exhausted. Her eyes were dry again, and she leaned back with a sigh. Maybe the familiarity of the setting would offer some comfort. After all, she was home again, where she wanted to be. This was part of what she had given up Jason for, so she might as well enjoy it.

The telephone rang and she pushed herself up like an invalid and walked slowly to the kitchen counter.

"Hi, Beth," she said in answer to her sister's greeting. "I just got in."

"You sound terrible," Beth said.

Lorna shrugged. "I feel terrible. It's all off between Jason and me, and I don't think he even understands why."

"Do you want to talk about it?"

"No," she decided. "It's too fresh."

After they hung up, Lorna carried her suitcase slowly up to her room. Of course each piece of clothing she removed from the bag carried a memory with it. That was only to be expected, she told herself sternly as she bundled everything up and tossed it into the clothes ham-

170

per. She was just delaying the inevitable by putting everything indiscriminately into the laundry. But it was the crumpled sheets of paper at the bottom of the suitcase that caused her the most pain.

She had no right to read them. Jason might not believe she had saved them only because she thought he might want them in the future. And anyway, he probably could recreate the poem from memory if he chose to. She should either send the papers to him right now, or throw them away. She smoothed them out carefully and sat down on the bed. It would be painful to read them, but the pain might be cleansing too.

A tear dropped on the paper as she read, and she wiped it away carefully. The poem was not, as she had half feared, a sexual memoir. In fact, it hardly related directly to her. It was a poem about being in love, a poem that any man or woman could read with pleasure and understanding. It expressed her own feelings for Jason as much as his feelings for her—the moments when something he did or said pierced her heart and filled her with tenderness, the moments of unexpected joy, the beauty of feeling at one with another person.

A sob tore at her throat and she dropped the papers on the floor to press a pillow against her chest. There was no comfort in the soft foam. There was no comfort anywhere. She hunched miserably on the edge of the bed, abandoning herself to her grief, until she had no more energy to cry. Then she lay back exhausted, still holding the pillow tightly, as if it could shield her from further hurt.

She remembered Jason's arms sliding around her waist as she stood at his kitchen sink. She could almost feel his chest against her back, his lips on her neck. She remembered sitting in the Jeep when he told her he loved her, and fresh tears rolled out of her eyes. She had never loved anyone the way she loved Jason, and now she had lost him because she wasn't self-sufficient enough. She would never again feel the security of his embrace, the excitement of his touch.

Her body seemed to be too heavy to move. Very slowly she picked up the poem from the floor. It deserved to be saved, and she would keep it until enough time had passed and she could send it back to Jason with an explanation. His bitterness wouldn't last forever, and someday he would regret the loss of this work. She put the papers neatly under some scarves in her dresser.

It was still early, but she decided to go to bed. She turned off the light, dropped her clothes on the floor, and fell onto the mattress. To help pass the time until she could fall asleep, she turned the radio to an all-night talk show, then rolled over on her side.

She got up early the next morning, having slept in brief snatches, and dressed carefully. Unfortunately, no amount of makeup could hide her swollen, circled eyes. She made hot cereal for breakfast, following some childhood precept that a hot breakfast would solve all problems, then left for work.

Fran came into her office the minute Lorna arrived at work, smiling and eager to hear any details that Lorna was willing to tell her. This was one of the moments she had been dreading, Lorna realized as she haltingly told Fran that she and Jason probably wouldn't see each other anymore.

"I just couldn't live with him in Vermont," she said, struggling to keep her voice from cracking. "I would have been completely alone most of the time, and the rest of the time I would have been alone with Jason, totally dependent on him for companionship."

Fran shook her head sympathetically. "From my position it sounds pretty good, but I see your point. It's a

172

little old-fashioned to expect a woman to give up her whole life for a man's convenience."

"It wasn't really like that," Lorna said. "He offered me a way of life he loved. He wanted to share his world with me. But I just couldn't accept it. It may be just the right way of life for him, but it isn't for me." She fished in her purse for a tissue.

"I know you don't believe it now, but you'll get over him in time, and then there'll be somebody else for you." Fran put her hand on Lorna's shoulder.

"I don't think I can ever love anyone else the way I love Jason," Lorna said, and Fran nodded.

"If you need company, just call."

Lorna blew her nose and pulled a stack of papers to the front of her desk. Maybe she could bury her feelings in her work.

As the summer term drew to a close, Lorna was discouraged about how little progress she had made in getting over Jason. To Beth and Fran she expressed complete confidence in her own recovery, but she knew she was empty inside. As she walked around the campus she kept her eyes lowered, and she avoided the window in her office, afraid of her own reaction if she should see Jason unexpectedly. Each time her telephone rang at home she had a moment of unreasoning hope that she would hear his deep voice once again. After all, it wasn't definite that they would never meet.

Near the end of the term she attended a performance of chamber music. As she scanned the audience at intermission her heart gave an unpleasant jump. There was Jason, clearly identifiable as he turned to talk to the woman next to him. She was a brunette, with long wavy hair and Mediterranean features. Her long gold earrings flashed with light as she threw her head back and laughed at something he said.

Lorna had never felt such jealousy. She was unable to stop watching the two of them. If she could have read their lips, she would have done so. She closed her eyes to block out the sight, and immediately envisioned the woman's strong brown arms clasping Jason passionately, her gold bracelets jingling. Lorna stood up and left, her back stiff with misery. Jason would never call.

"Want to take up jogging with me?" Fran asked the next day.

"Am I starting to get fat?" Lorna inspected the waist-line of her dress.

"No, but you seem pretty tense lately," Fran said, "and jogging is supposed to be good for that. For another thing, I hear you meet all kinds of wonderful men that way. I've been thinking of taking it up myself, but I don't have the courage to do it alone."

Lorna hesitated. "It's a thought, I guess. But maybe I'd be better off playing more tennis. Sorry if I've been gloomy."

Fran put her arm around Lorna's shoulders. "You've just lost a little of your bounce, that's all."

She'd have to do something to snap out of her misery, Lorna decided, if she hadn't been hiding it as well as she thought. The staff family picnic was approaching, and she promised herself that now, as in years past, she would abandon herself to a day of softball, three-legged races, and pie-eating contests. She had always loved this event, and she would love it again this year if it killed her.

On the day of the picnic she dressed in a pair of brilliant blue shorts and a matching rugby shirt. A good deal of thought had gone into her lunch, since the competition over who had brought the most exotic and sophisticated food was one of the unsung highlights of the day. She had made enough pâté to feed the entire population of California, she thought, and she carefully wrapped a third of it to take to the picnic. The cucumber soup was well chilled, and she poured it carefully into an insulated bottle. A small loaf of French bread, some silverware and plates, and she was ready.

As she found a shady parking place at the park she realized that she was honestly looking forward to having a good time. She sat down on a quilt with Fran and several other friends from the administration building and accepted a cold bottle of sparkling mineral water. Some children were already rowing out onto the small lake, and a game of Frisbee was in progress on a grassy lawn nearby. She lay back contentedly and looked up through the leaves of the huge magnolia tree that shaded their picnic spot and filled the air with the lemony scent of its blossoms.

"Isn't that Jason Coulter?" one of the secretaries asked, and Lorna took a deep breath.

"He's wonderful, isn't he?" someone else responded. "I'd love to meet him."

"You know him, don't you, Lorna?"

"Yes."

"Could you introduce us?" Karin asked.

"He's really very pleasant," Lorna said. "I think if you introduce yourselves, he'll be happy to chat with you. After all, he's standing by himself. You don't need a formal introduction to talk to him."

"I'd still rather be introduced," Karin said wistfully.

Lorna gazed at the sky for a moment. "Okay," she said with a sigh. "Come with me."

Jason was standing alone, watching the children on the lake. Even the back of his head was achingly familiar. The set of his shoulders reminded her irresistibly of the times she had walked up behind him and curved her arms around his waist. She could remember the texture of his shirt against her cheek, its clean, faintly soapy scent.

She paused, aware that Linda and Karin were waiting expectantly. Jason hadn't called her. She could assume that he didn't want to see her again. But surely he could have guessed she might be at the picnic, so he would hardly be astonished to see her now. With a trembling finger she touched his arm lightly. He turned, then seemed to pull away slightly when he realized it was she. Looking into his dark eyes, she felt as if she were about to lose her balance.

He didn't smile at all. He was almost frowning at her, and Lorna's plans for a cheery, superficial greeting disintegrated as she studied the familiar planes of his face. There were shadows under his eyes, taut skin around his cheekbones that she didn't remember, and she longed to smooth his face with her fingertips. She should have found the courage to call him, to suggest that they spend a few more weeks together. If she had, she wouldn't be standing here now, three feet away from him, struggling to hide her emotions.

"Hello, Lorna," he said finally, and she couldn't bear to meet his eyes.

"Linda and Karin wanted to meet you," she said quickly, hoping her voice wouldn't falter. "They're fans of yours who work with me."

"I'm very happy to meet you." Jason turned immediately to Karin and, as Karin put her hand out, Lorna turned to walk away. "I'll talk to you later," Jason called, and she flapped a hand noncommittally at him, knowing he was just being polite.

The softball game was starting up, and Lorna gratefully took her place on the women's team. She was the third batter to strike out, to good-natured *boos* from the observers, and she shrugged theatrically. "What do you

176

expect from someone who plays only once a year?" she called over her shoulder as she walked into the outfield, and as she turned back she saw Jason standing on the sideline watching her.

The men's team won the game embarrassingly quickly, and the participants returned to their lunches, vowing a rematch after they had eaten.

"May I sit with you?" Lorna froze, unable to raise her eyes from the pâté she was unwrapping. She hadn't really expected to hear that deep, rich voice again.

"Yes, please do," she said, and wished she could tell him how much she wanted him there. "Would you like some of this?" she asked, and Jason nodded.

"Actually, I heard that you pack the best lunches of anyone here, so I've been waiting for my opportunity to cadge some food."

Somehow, everyone else who had been sitting on the faded quilt seemed to have found another place to go, and the two of them were alone.

"Can we go somewhere and talk for a few minutes?"

Lorna looked around blankly. "I guess we could walk across the park," she said finally. "That would give us a little privacy."

They stood up together and she tightened her lips to keep them from trembling as they walked through the picnickers and down a gentle slope to a bench that was nearly hidden in a copse of trees. They sat down and turned a little awkwardly to face each other. There were no other people in sight.

"I've been thinking about you," Jason said.

"I've thought about you too." Lorna looked down at her hands. "And I've missed you." There was a lump in her throat that threatened to choke her.

Jason shifted to move a little closer. "I've realized that

177

we had a special rapport, something between us most people never find. I really don't want to give that up."

"I'll always love you," Lorna said softly, and he gripped her hand. "But I just can't promise to do something I'm sure would end in misery for us both."

Jason was quiet for a few moments. "Maybe I don't really have to be in Vermont," he said finally. "Just someplace where I can find peace and quiet, where I know I can get away from everything."

"The trouble is, I don't want to get that far away. I'd end up resenting your work, wanting you to keep me company and amuse me because I was alone. I need to be near a college campus, somewhere where I can work at a job I have experience in and enjoy. Even if we decided to have children later. . . ."

"I understand." His voice was very tender, and Lorna suddenly thought that perhaps he really did understand.

"Sometimes I've thought," she began, not meeting his eyes, "that maybe we could find a small college town, a little place that's tucked away but that still would have the job opportunities I need. We could live rather far away—I don't mind commuting if I don't have to ford a creek twice a day. If you moved to the village, for instance, maybe then . . ."

Jason's hand moved to the back of her neck, stroking her hair for a moment before he pulled her gently toward him. Their lips met, very softly at first, and she felt a rush of emotion that filled her eyes with tears. His hand moved up and down her back, his lips moved sweetly against hers, and one large tear rolled down her cheek and rested against his skin.

He pulled away slightly, then traced the salty track with his lips as his hands cupped her face. Her breath was coming a little faster and she leaned toward him farther to renew the kiss, one hand softly caressing his thigh. His hand dropped to her breast and she sighed deeply, pressing against his palm. She'd never get over him, never be immune to these feelings.

"I love you very much," he whispered, his breath tickling her hair. "Can you give me some time to think this through?"

Lorna nodded, her hand still moving on his thigh. If only they had gone back to her house, she thought, resting her head against his shoulder as he stroked her hair. She was past the point of protecting herself. They could have made love again, even if it were for the last time, and she would have that much more to remember. Right now, sitting on the bench, she wanted him more than she had ever wanted anyone, more than she could have imagined. And the faint trembling of his hand against her cheek told her that he felt it too.

"Kiss me," she pleaded, and he bent to her immediately, one finger tracing her ear as his tongue explored her mouth. His hand was on her bare thigh then, slipping under the cuff of her shorts, and she moaned as he stroked the soft skin.

"This has to stop," he said in a husky voice, and pressed his lips into the hollow of her throat, "before we get arrested." He kissed each breast lightly, his breath hot even through the layers of fabric, and then with a sigh he sat up.

They looked at each other, flushed and disheveled, and then Jason touched her lips lightly with one finger. "I think I'll just walk back this way to my car." He stood up, gesturing to the road that ran around the park. "I'll see you."

"See you," she echoed, and watched him walk away. She felt bereft, but she knew she'd done all she could. She wanted him desperately, but she loved him too much to ruin both their lives. Surely they could find their way to a solution to the problem if Jason wanted it as much as she did. The ball was in his court now, and she would have to wait until she heard from him again.

CHAPTER ELEVEN

Her telephone rang two days later just as she was taking her first sip of coffee, and it startled her into spilling several drops down her blouse. "Damn," she said as she picked up the phone with her left hand and heard a deep chuckle before she'd had time to say hello.

"I was afraid I might be calling too early, and apparently my fears were well-founded."

"No, I just spilled my coffee." Lorna sat down carefully in a chair. Was he calling to tell her his decision?

"I've decided to go back to Vermont," he began, and she closed her eyes briefly. "Only for a few days," he added hastily. "Whatever you say, I do my best thinking there, and I need to think about us."

"Are the students besieging you here?"

He sighed. "Not really. I just want to get away. I have only the last class meeting to conduct, and the final papers won't be due until then, so my presence isn't really required here."

"I see." It was nearly time for him to leave for good anyway. Most likely he'd settle in once he got there and decide not to come back.

"Maybe I'm running away. Maybe not." His voice was

heavy and for a moment she longed to put her arms around him.

"I'll talk to you in a few days then," she said after a brief silence.

"This is not just my decision, you know." His voice seemed lighter now, and almost tender. She pressed the receiver tightly against her ear. "I don't know right now what I want or what I can give you, but I recognize that you're under no obligation to accept any offer I make. It may be that things have gone too far wrong between us. Maybe we can't go back."

"I don't know." Her voice was trembling, and she bit her lip.

"I'll call you." A sudden click told her that he had hung up, and she carefully replaced her own receiver. She sat in the chair as if she had been frozen, her hand still resting on the telephone, her eyes staring unfocused out the kitchen window. How long would she have to wait, and for what? Possibly this reprieve was only temporary. Shaking her head as if to clear her thoughts, she stood up and walked briskly out to her car. It was time to leave for work.

She made it through that day and the next one somehow, keeping herself so busy she had almost no time to think of Jason. Brisk tennis games after work, late suppers, and nights spent painting the upstairs hallway kept her tired enough to sleep and filled the hours until his return.

If he did return, that is. When she allowed herself to think of him, she alternated between a delicious fantasy of an agreeable compromise and a conviction that once in Vermont, he would decide he never wanted to leave. If he did come back, and offered anything at all, she could live with, she would take it, she decided. Jason was such a unique individual, she could never imagine finding another man she could love as strongly.

Her mind flew to an image of herself locked in his arms, the two of them in a tight embrace. Their bodies would flow together and they would stand that way for several minutes without kissing or caressing, each simply enjoying the warmth of the other's presence. Then, at last, their lips would touch, Jason's hands would begin to move down her back, and her fingers would stroke the back of his head and his neck. Her knees would weaken, she would feel the familiar loosening of her thighs . . .

She wrenched her thoughts brutally back to reality. Perhaps she would never see Jason again. He might telephone, either from Vermont or from the cottage, to tell her he was not able to compromise. And then she would be back where she had been before the picnic. Surely nothing could be worse than what she had already suffered, except a marriage to Jason that would end in more heartbreak and bitterness.

She had dinner with Beth and her family the next night, and was unexpectedly cheerful. She ate her cold tomato soup with relish, and was equally enthusiastic about the avocados stuffed with crab.

"I'm glad to see you're feeling better," Beth whispered as they loaded the dishwasher in the kitchen. "You really seem to be your old self again. Has he gone back to Vermont?"

"Yes, but he may come back in a few days. I talked to him a little at the college picnic."

Beth frowned. "I hope he didn't lead you on again. I've been tempted to call him up and say horrible things to him for breaking your heart."

Lorna carefully put a blue flowered dinner plate between two plastic prongs. "He didn't really do anything to me that I didn't do to him also. It was no one's fault."

Beth put her hands on her hips, looking very maternal in a ruffly blue apron. "You're still in love with him, aren't you?"

Lorna nodded. "Someday I'll tell you all about it. But I know I've never . . ." Feeling a sob catch in her throat, she stopped abruptly. "I'd better go."

It was a lonely drive home, although the sun had not yet set, and once she had unlocked her front door Lorna tossed her purse on the sofa and stood in the middle of the room, wondering how she could occupy the next few hours until she was tired enough to go to bed. She should have stayed at Beth's. The doorbell rang and she started nervously, her hand to her mouth. It was probably the paper boy, she decided. No one else was likely to call unannounced so late in the evening.

She opened the door a crack, her lips already forming her request that he wait while she got her purse, and saw Jason standing on the step, dressed in jeans and a dark blue sweater.

"I just got in and I wanted to see you right away," he said quietly. "May I come in?"

"Of course." Lorna felt her heartbeat quicken and the color rush to her cheeks. She realized she was blocking the door and backed away. "Would you like something to drink?"

He shook his head with a rueful smile. "No, I'd like you to sit down with me and listen to what I have to say."

She sat down next to him, feeling a little shaky.

"I hardly stayed in Vermont at all. The house seemed so empty without you, I realized I didn't want to be there alone. I couldn't write either." He hesitated, and Lorna shifted slightly to face him more directly.

"I'm sorry, if somehow I've ruined your house for you. It's such a beautiful place."

"You haven't ruined it for me, just made me realize its limitations. It's fine for a brief vacation, but no normal adult should live there alone year-round unless he or she has decided to give up on civilization."

A stab of hope made Lorna gnaw on her thumbnail.

"Anyway," he went on, his eyes were dark, "I began to see that you were right. I was doing some of what I've accused you of doing. I was trying to seal myself off from everyone except you. It was easy enough to pride myself on how much I'd learned and matured when there was no one around to challenge the way I'd chosen to solve my problems. Maybe we all need to be around people to learn about ourselves. Anyway, whether I like it or not, I can't go back to being a hermit. And since you're so happy here with your job and your friends, I see no reason to uproot you just to save my pride. A few weeks ago I got an offer from the state university of a tenured position here. I've decided to accept."

"I'm glad." Lorna looked at him, her mind spinning.

"And I've brought you a present." He stood and walked out the front door to his car while she sat numbly on the sofa and waited.

"It's not a ring." With a grin he presented her with a Chinese porcelain bowl filled with potting soil and a number of tiny, delicate plants. "This is to replace your cactus garden on the windowsill," he said smiling. "If you so choose, of course. We've both had enough of holding other people off with our prickly exteriors. Now it's time for us to be a little more tender and vulnerable, like these little plants."

Lorna took the bowl without a word and carried it into the kitchen. "Shall I throw this away?" she asked, picking up the bowl of cacti.

"It might be premature," Jason said deliberately.

185

"Maybe you want to tuck it in a closet somewhere, where you can get it out later if you want to."

"No." Unceremoniously, she opened the cupboard below the sink and tossed the cactus bowl in the garbage can. "There." She dusted her hands before picking up the new bowl and placing it carefully on the windowsill.

"Will you still have me?" Jason asked softly, and she nodded once, stepping into his arms.

"I didn't think you would come back," she whispered, her face buried in the hollow of his shoulder. He stroked her hair so softly she could barely feel the movement, and she curved her body into his, enjoying the familiar scent of his skin, the feeling of his arms holding her close against him. She took a deep breath and pulled a little away from him to look up smilingly into his eyes, loving the curve of his mouth, the faint creases in his forehead, but most of all the look she saw in his eyes, somehow more tender and caressing than it had even been before.

He kissed her once, the pressure of his lips very light and delicate, and she moved her hands down his back, molding her palms around the muscles she could discern under his sweater. With one finger he traced her cheekbones, smiling into her eyes.

"Let's just take things slowly," he said huskily, "and make sure we know what we're doing. I've been alone so long, you may find me impossible in the long run."

"I need to be sure you're not sacrificing your work for me," Lorna said, reluctantly pulling away from him. "Will you still write?"

"I don't know." He sat down on the sofa and she sat in the other corner, turning sideways to face him. "I'll be teaching, which I expect to enjoy, and I thought this might be the time for me to start on the great American novel."

"I don't want to feel responsible for depriving the

world of a poet," Lorna said in dismay. "Are you sure you can't write poetry here?"

"I don't think I can write poetry anywhere right now. I used the students and autograph hounds as an excuse, but the love poem seems to have been the last poem I had in me. It's like the conclusion of a cycle. I'm ready to move on to something different."

"I saved the poem for you," Lorna confessed. "I took it out of the garbage."

"By the time I had it written I could have reproduced it from memory." He squeezed her hand tightly. "But it was nice of you to rescue it. Throwing it away was an overdramatic gesture on my part, I'm afraid. Did you like the poem?"

"It was wonderful." Lorna stood up suddenly. "We should do something to celebrate, don't you think?" She twirled around. "I feel like dancing or singing or something ridiculous."

He gave a soft laugh. "Come back and sit down and maybe we can think of a proper celebration."

With a smile she sank down very close to him on the sofa, her arms around his neck as if they belonged there, and as their lips met she allowed herself to sink back into the cushions. It had been too long since they'd been together, and now his nearness made her head swim a little.

"Don't ever go away from me again," she said softly, sliding her hands under his shirt and sweater. The skin of his back was very warm and smooth, and she ran her fingertips silkily over his shoulder blades and down his spine. His lips moved against hers insistently, coaxing her, and she drew a deep breath of air into her lungs. His fingers were at the buttons of her dress and she leaned back farther, sliding over until they were lying together on the sofa.

"I'd almost forgotten how beautiful you are," he murmured, his breath torturing her naked breasts, and she stroked his hair as his lips and tongue made her feverish with desire. By now he seemed to know all her body's secrets, her hidden wishes, and she moaned in anticipation as his hand caressed first her knee, then her thigh.

"I've never stopped thinking about you, not for a minute," he whispered, carefully pulling off her sandals. She lifted her hips as he pulled off the rest of her clothes, and watched him as he swiftly undressed. As she pulled him next to her, embracing him tightly, she was suddenly reminded of the evening months ago when on the same sofa she had stopped him from making love to her.

"Would you like to make me yours?" she asked, giving his earlobe a sharp nip.

"Forever," he said, holding her even closer, and she pressed her lips fiercely to his.

All-new **Candlelight Newsletter**

An exceptional, *free* offer awaits readers of Dell's incomparable Candlelight Ecstasy and Supreme Romances.

Subscribe to our all-new CANDLELIGHT NEWSLETTER and you will receive—at absolutely no cost to you—exciting, exclusive information about today's finest romance novels and novelists. You'll be part of a select group to receive sneak previews of upcoming Candlelight Romances, well in advance of publication.

You'll also go behind the scenes to "meet" our Ecstasy and Supreme authors, learning firsthand where they get their ideas and how they made it to the top. News of author appearances and events will be detailed, as well. And contributions from the Candlelight editor will give you the inside scoop on how she makes her decisions about what to publish—and how *you* can try your hand at writing an Ecstasy or Supreme.

You'll find all this and more in Dell's CANDLELIGHT NEWSLETTER. And best of all, *it costs you nothing.* That's right! It's Dell's way of thanking our loyal Candlelight readers and of adding another dimension to your reading enjoyment.

Just fill out the coupon below, return it to us, and look forward to receiving the first of many CANDLELIGHT NEWSLETTERS—overflowing with the kind of excitement that only enhances our romances!

Fans of
JAYNE CASTLE
rejoice—
this is her
biggest
and best
romance
yet!

From California's glittering gold coast, to the rustic islands of Puget Sound, Jayne Castle's longest, most ambitious novel to date sweeps readers into the corporate world of multimillion dollar real estate schemes—and the very *private* world of executive lovers. Mixing business with pleasure, they make passion *their* bottom line.

384 pages $3.95

Don't forget
Candlelight Ecstasies,
for Jayne Castle's
other romances!